MYSTERY AT MIRROR LAKE

Tovi:
Hope you enjoy
the Read!
Myra Galloway
6/11/2022

Myra Galloway

ISBN 978-1-64471-993-0 (Paperback)
ISBN 978-1-64471-994-7 (Digital)

Covenant Books, Inc.
11661 Hwy 707
Murrells Inlet, SC 29576
www.covenantbooks.com

DEDICATION

To my sister, Jackie Hopskin, who inspired me to become an author, and to all the would-be writers of the world, dreams are just reality in the making.

CHARACTERS

Helen O'Keefe Coleman—fifty-six years old from Twin City, Georgia, starting a new life back in her hometown, Mirror Lake, North Carolina, to be close to her elderly mother. She is opening an art and antiquities gallery.

Denton Gage—fifty-five years old, widower. Moved from New York after losing his wife in the September 11, 2001, terrorist attacks. He is the new sheriff of Mirror Lake.

Margaret O'Keefe—forty-eight years old, Helen's sister, lives in Atlanta, Georgia, financial advisor, single workaholic.

Henry Mason—mayor of Mirror Lake, North Carolina.

Gordon Grover—owner of the G&G Bar and Grill.

Mr. J. Sommeren—from Istanbul, Turkey, in imports/exports, with terrorist links.

Mr. Ameer Amjad—business partner with Mr. Sommeren, with terrorist links.

Supporting Characters

Pat and David Martin—sister and brother-in-law of Helen and Margaret, horse farmers in Cumming, Georgia.

Melonie and Donald Steedwell—sister and brother-in-law of Helen and Margaret. Melonie is head nurse in local hospital, and Donald is postmaster in a small South Georgia town.

Mildred O'Keefe—mother of Helen, Margaret, Pat, and Melonie.

Jack Abrams with Homeland Security out of Washington DC.

Billy Bob Johnson—local contractor and ex-military.

PROLOGUE

September 11, 2001, news reports all over the networks come across in disbelief. "I can't believe my eyes. There is another plane. It's going to hit the North Tower. Oh my god!" Within an hour and half both, towers have collapsed—the world is stunned.

Detective Denton Gage, one of New York's finest, rushes to the scene. Fear is welling up inside him as he performs his duty. His thoughts are on his wife and the North Tower. All he can do is hope that she was late going into work.

In a small town, Mirror Lake, North Carolina, fifty-six-year-old Helen Coleman sits in her mother's kitchen, having coffee and watching the nightmare unfold in New York. Her heart aches as she thinks of the sorrow and pain many will feel for love ones lost in this horrific event, for she, too, has—only six months earlier—lost her husband to a sudden heart attack.

In the story told in the following pages, the lives of these two people—Helen Coleman and Denton Gage, as well as the small town of Mirror Lake—unfolds with mystery and romance.

CHAPTER 1

April 3, 2002, Helen Coleman looks over the small building she is about to renovate for her new Arts and Antiquities Gallery. It's a building that has long since belonged to her family—the O'Keefe's. When in walks Henry Mason, the mayor of Mirror Lake.

"Helen," says Henry as he reaches for her hand. "I can't tell you how happy we are to have you back home"—Helen just smiles—"and the excitement that you bring with you with the new Arts and Antiquities Gallery is over whelming."

As Henry lets go of her hand, Helen says, "I hope that your excitement isn't too premature. We have a ways to go before opening. There will be a lot of work just getting ready."

As Helen trails off, Henry jumps right back in. "Yes, I understand. But this type of business is just what Mirror Lake needs, with all the newcomer's attracted to the area for the resort."

With Henry is Denton Gage, the new sheriff of Mirror Lake. Helen looks over at Denton as Henry doesn't miss a beat. "Where is my manners. Helen, this is Denton Gage, our new sheriff. Denton, this is Helen Coleman."

Henry pauses and looks at Helen with a question mark look on his face.

"That's Helen O'Keefe Coleman." Helen finishes as Henry turns a little red-faced.

"Helen's family has been a part of Mirror Lake since the beginning. Her father was the first real mayor of Mirror Lake, Charles O'Keefe." As Henry continues, Helen just smiles at Denton.

Denton smiles back with the thought that Helen sure has a nice smile. "I believe that was around 1945, wasn't it?"

Henry looking back at Helen. "Yes, it was just after he came home from the war."

Denton picked up, "What branch of service?"

"He was air force fighter pilot."

Before Helen could say more, Henry cuts in, "Yes, he was one of Mirror Lake's heroes."

"Oh"—Denton looks at Helen—"I would love to hear the story sometime, perhaps over coffee."

As Henry starts for the door, he said, "Denton and I've a meeting with the chamber of commerce in about twenty minutes."

As Denton nods, he said, "I'm sure I'll be seeing you around."

Helen just nods and smiles. "Yes, I'm sure."

CHAPTER 2

As Helen takes stock of the building, it had been a type of old general store once. It has old hardwood floors and old double doors at the entrance. When you walk in, the middle is open. Toward the back of the store is a stairwell leading to the second-floor mezzanine of sorts.

After looking over the building, Helen decides it will not need much renovation: redo the hardwood floors and put in glassed in cabinets, mirrored walls with special lighting for affect and a tables-and-easel area on the mezzanine for displays. The hard part was going to be the art and antiquities that will go into the gallery. Helen's thoughts go to her sister, Margaret, in Atlanta. *I'll have to give her a call. She will have some good ideas and hopefully some good contacts.* As Helen reaches for her cell phone, it rings.

"Hi, sis," Margaret says with a smile on her face. "How goes it?"

"Well, you'll never believe it. I'm standing in the middle of the old general store and was just about to give you a call."

"Really, not having second thoughts, are you?" But before Helen could answer, Margaret continues, "Because I've some great ideas for the gallery."

"Oh really, I was hoping you would," Helen says.

"I thought I would come up this weekend and see Mom and look over the place, and we could talk."

As Margaret finishes, Helen says, "Does that mean I'll see you bright and early Saturday morning?"

With a laugh, Margaret says, "Well, you know me not too early. But I'll see you by noon. Gotta go. Love you, sis."

As Margaret hangs up, Helen whispers in the already dead line, "Love you too."

Later that afternoon, Henry Mason sits at a table with Gordon Grover at the G&G Bar and Grill. Gordon looks over at Henry and says, "Well, how was the meeting with the chamber of commerce?"

As Henry swirls the ice in his glass of gin, he says, "Well, same old same old. This town just doesn't get it."

"What? They still don't want outside influence for new business?" Gordon just stares at Henry.

"Well, they're just going to have to move into the twenty-first century and realize without some outside influence, This town is just going to dry up and blow away," says Henry with a little anger in his voice.

"Well, with these new fellows wanting to buy into the resort, that should help," Gordon says with a bit of a smile.

"Not enough," Henry continues, "we have to show them that it's worth their investment. Then maybe they will bring in some of their friends. You know some of that oil money from some of their Middle East buddies." Henry just smiles.

CHAPTER 3

Meanwhile, back in Atlanta, Margaret is on her way to a lunch meeting with her new clients, Mr. J. Sommeren and Mr. Ameer Amjad. As she walks into the tea room in the main lobby of The Ritz Carlton, looking around for her clients, she feels a tap on her shoulder. She turns to face a middle-aged man of Middle Eastern descent.

"Mr. Sommeren, I presume," Margaret ask.

"Yes, and you must be Ms. O'Keefe."

"Yes, but please, call me Margaret."

"As you wish, Margaret," says Mr. Sommeren. "Shall we sit?" ask Mr. Sommeren.

"Yes, let's get comfortable," Margaret replies.

As they make their way to their table, Margaret asks, "Is Mr. Ameer Amjad with you today?"

"No, he sends his regrets. He had other business to attend to."

Margaret's thoughts wonder briefly to what other business that could be. Since last speaking with Mr. Sommeren, he had made it sound as though neither gentleman had acquaintances in the states, let alone in the Atlanta area. As Mr. Sommeren starts to speak, her thoughts fade.

"Ms. O'Keefe—Margaret—have you had an opportunity to consider our last conversation?"

"Yes, I have! I've looked into several investment opportunities I think you might be interested in. From real estate to restaurants, but the one I think that may interest you the most is a small arts and antiquities gallery! It's located about 135 miles north of Atlanta in an up and coming mountain resort town called Mirror Lake. It's just located over the Georgia state line in North Carolina."

Before Margaret could go on, Mr. Sommeren's eyes seem to sparkle as he says, "Please, tell me more."

"As I said, it's a small town, but the resort is growing, as well as the town. But I feel it will be a good investment for you and a great way for you to bring your arts and culture to this part of the world. Also I would like to point out that many of the elite from not only Georgia but all over the US seem to be attracted to the area."

"Sounds very good. I'll, of course, talk with Mr. Amjad and go over this with him."

As Margaret hands Mr. Sommeren a folder with different investment outlines in it, Mr. Sommeren continues, "I feel Mr. Amjad will like to see this little arts and antiquities gallery, as well as the resort."

Margaret smiles. "I'll be happy to take you there and show you around."

Little does Margaret know, her new clients are already acquainted with the resort at Mirror Lake! Mr. Sommeren heads back to the suite of rooms that he and Mr. Amjad share on the tenth floor of The Ritz Carlton; he can't help but smile. He feels like everything is coming together better than they had hoped. This means they're ahead of schedule. He can't wait until he speaks with Mr. Amjad to see how his day has gone. Later that evening, over dinner, Mr. Sommeren and Mr. Amjad couldn't believe their good fortune. Allah had truly blessed them.

CHAPTER 4

In an out of the way little café, just north of the city of Asheville, North Carolina, Henry Mason sits and talks with his new acquaintance, Mr. Ameer Amjad, from somewhere in the Middle East. Henry really doesn't care where the gentleman is from. He is more interested in the money he brings to invest in their mountain resort. Henry doesn't even think anything about the mysterious way in which Mr. Amjad came to know about Mirror Lake, or why he would want to invest in Mirror Lake Resort, nor does it bother him that this person he knows nothing about is also interested in a parcel of land, covering over three hundred acres. The parcel is way up in a very secluded area of the North Carolina mountains and has been in Henry's family for years. It was once used as a controlled fox hunting club. It has several buildings on the property, and the whole area is fenced in.

For Henry, the only thing he can see and understand is money. Mr. Amjad says, "I'm very happy with the hunt club. I've always enjoyed the sport of hunting, but never have I had the opportunity to be in control of the hunt. I'm ready to sign an agreement to lease the hunt club for one year with second-year option. How does $300,000 for the first year with an extra $200,000 for the second year if we decide to go with two years."

Henry sits staring in disbelief. He can't believe his luck. Here is this man he met just about a month ago when in Las Vegas—by pure chance—offering a deal of a life time. Mr. Amjad and Mr. Sommeren were in Vegas, sitting at the same blackjack table when they struck up a conversation with Henry. Little did Henry know that their little meeting was not by chance! Mr. Ameer Amjad already had every detail worked out before ever going to Las Vegas.

As Helen, walking across the street, headed toward the tax accessors office, Denton pulls up next to her. "Well, hello, Ms. Coleman, how are you today?"

"Mr. Gage, isn't it?"

"Yes, but please call me Denton."

"Yes, well then by all means call me Helen, and I'm doing fine."

"Huh."

"The answer to your question, I'm doing fine." Helen gives a little laugh.

"Well then, are you up for a cup of coffee?" Denton asks as he smiles.

Helen says, "I'm sorry, but I was just on my way into the tax office to obtain some permits for the renovation of my new gallery. Perhaps a rain check?"

"Okay, I'll hold you to that," says Denton.

Helen can't help but smile to herself and think this could be an interesting friendship as Denton drives away.

CHAPTER 5

Henry was sitting at his desk, going over the events of the day, when his phone rang.

"Henry, where have you been?" says Gordon.

"Huh?" says Henry.

"I've been trying to reach you all day, and your office just said you were out. I couldn't get anything on your cell."

Henry says, "I was just attending to some business." Henry was not sure how much he wanted to share with Gordon information or money. However, he did owe Gordon money. After all, Gordon had put up more than half of the money needed to set up the hunt club some years back. And it had never begun to pay the bills. Plus, Henry really wanted to tell someone of his good fortune.

"Henry, are you there? What's wrong with you? Are you sick or something?" asks Gordon.

"No, I'm not sick! But I do have some good news," Henry states then stops. "I'll be over in a bit, and I'll fill you in."

"Okay, see you later," Gordon replies.

Henry says, "Throw me the biggest New York strip on the grill you got…and pull your best bottle of scotch. We got some celebrating to do."

Saturday morning, April 6, Helen gets up to a light snowfall. She thinks about Margaret coming from Atlanta and hopes the weather doesn't present a problem. She is very excited to hear more about Margaret's ideas for the gallery.

In Atlanta, where it's cold but clear, Margaret is preparing to hit the road. She's always loved the drive from Atlanta to Mirror Lake. The scenery is so beautiful and serene; it's always a great stress release for her. Also she can't wait to tell Helen about Mr. Sommeren and

Mr. Ameer Amjad and their eagerness to see and hear more about the gallery. This—she hopes—will be a great source of some really unique and priceless exhibits for the gallery.

Just about the same time, Margaret's phone rings, and it's Helen. She is calling to let Margaret know about the weather. Margaret says, "Hi, sis, what's going on?"

Helen, in response, says, "Wanted to let you know, it's snowing up here, but they're not excepting more than an inch or so, and it's supposed to warm up tonight and melt by noon tomorrow."

Margaret says, "Thanks for the info, but I've already checked it out."

Helen says, "I should have known you couldn't afford to get stuck in Mirror Lake with your busy life," and gives a little laugh.

Margaret, in return, says, "You know me well."

CHAPTER 6

Margaret arrives at Mirror Lake by about 12:30 p.m., and she goes straight to her mother's, Mildred O'Keefe's house. She walks into the kitchen where Helen and her mother sit having coffee. She sits and visits with her mom and Helen until Helen says, "Let's go look at the store. See what you think."

Helen and Margaret head out toward town. Now Mirror Lake isn't a large town by any means. Main Street consists of several different shops. There are a couple of boutiques, a florist, a bookstore, a coffee shop, and several eateries, as well as an ice cream polar, and of course, the old general store where the arts and antiquities gallery is going to be at.

As Helen and Margaret get to the store, Denton Gage walks up. He's just come from the coffee shop. Denton says, "Good afternoon, Helen."

Helen turns at the sound of his voice and smiles. "Good afternoon to you, sheriff."

Denton smiles back and says it's turning out to be a fine day. Helen just stands there for a minute when Margaret says, "Hi, I'm Margaret, Helen's sister. You have to forgive my sister's manners. She just forgets sometimes."

Helen says, "I'm so sorry, please forgive me," as she looks at Margaret. Helen continues, "Margaret is from Atlanta, just up for the weekend. She is helping me with the planning and designing of the gallery."

Denton says, "That must be nice to have someone to help with ideas and such."

Helen responds, "Yes, it is, and she has good contacts that I hope will help with filling the gallery. Of course, we also plan to use some things from local artist as well."

Denton says, "That's nice. It's always good to help out your neighbors and fellow art lovers." Denton continues and nods. "Ladies, I need to get back to work. Nice to meet you, Margaret, and always a pleasure to see you, Helen."

As Denton walks off, Helen and Margaret go into the store. Once inside, Margaret turns to Helen and says while waving her hand in front of her face, "Wow, he is hot. And I think he just might like what he sees in you."

Helen's face turns red, and she says, "Oh, you are silly. He is just being nice."

Margaret says, "Okay, if you say so, but I think there could be something there."

Helen says, "I've too much to do for that kind of nonsense." Helen walks in the middle of the store and asks, "So what do you think."

Margaret says, "I think it can be turned into something special."

As Helen walks through, she is talking with her hands, saying how she wants to redo the floors and put in mirrored walls with special lighting for effect and glass cabinets and tables and easels on the mezzanine. Margaret tells her, "That sounds great! Let's go over to the coffee shop and talk about what kind of things you want to go into the gallery, and I'll tell you what I've found out and what I have in mind."

CHAPTER 7

Helen and Margaret are having a cup of coffee in the local coffee shop while Margaret is telling Helen about some new clients of hers, a Mr. J. Sommeren and a Mr. Ameer Amjad from Turkey. She is explaining to Helen how they're excited about Mirror Lake and the gallery and how they're looking for investments. Margaret continues to explain to Helen how she plans to bring them up to Mirror Lake to show them around and to see the gallery. Margaret says they're very excited about bringing some of their arts and culture to the area. Also, they're looking forward to the resort.

Helen says, "That sounds great. However, do you really want to bring them up before I get the renovation done?"

Margaret says, "Well, how long do you think that will take?"

Helen says, "I've already gotten the permits, and I plan on contacting Billy Bob, who is a local contractor, on Monday to see if he can get started right away. I think the thing that will take the longest will be getting the cabinets and lighting and getting them installed."

Margaret says, "So may be in about two weeks?"

Helen replies, "Well, the renovations may be done but not sure what kind of display we'll have. I've already talked with some of the local artist regarding some art, pottery, and even some metal artwork. If we can get that part up and running and ready to sell, then just maybe we could really have this galley looking halfway professional."

Margaret says, "Sounds like a plan to me."

They go back to their mom's house and enjoy the rest of the weekend.

Meanwhile, Denton is sitting at his desk and thinking about Helen. It has been a while since a woman, other than his wife, has been on his mind like Helen. She actually reminds him of his late wife in a strange kind of way. Helen is strong and very independent just like his wife was. He can't help but let it bring fond memories to mind. So far, this new beginning for him seems to be good. As long as he stays focused and not dwell on the bad memories.

Margret is back at work in Atlanta on Monday morning. She is in her office at Gilpin, Grays, and Connor Financial Group, which looks out over Peachtree Street. She is going over the investment plans she gave to Mr. Sommeren, wondering if he had gone over them with Mr. Amjad. Margaret is anxious to hear from them. She really hopes this is going to be good for Helen and the gallery. She knows that this is really important to Helen and wants to help as much as she can.

CHAPTER 8

As Margaret is working, her phone rings, and it's Mr. Sommeren. He says, "Good morning, Margaret. Mr. Sommeren here. I hope you had a good weekend."

Margaret replies, "Yes, indeed, thanks for asking. I hope you and Mr. Amjad did as well. Also I'm interested in what Mr. Amjad had to say about the outline of investments I provided for you?"

Mr. Sommeren says, "He was as excited as I was, especially regarding the arts and antiquities gallery in Mirror Lake. Mr. Amjad loves art and has longed to share our art and culture with the world. It's important to him for the rest of the world to see and appreciate our culture."

Margaret says, "I'm so glad to hear that. I was in Mirror Lake this past weekend and spoke with Helen Coleman regarding the gallery and when it might open. It looks to be about two to four weeks before it's ready. I would like to take you and Mr. Amjad up to Mirror Lake and show you around and meet Mrs. Coleman but prefer it be after the gallery is open."

"That's fine, we have to be back in Turkey on business this week, and most likely would not be back in Atlanta for at least three weeks. Also Mr. Amjad would like to know if it will be possible for some of the artwork to be just exhibits and not necessarily for sale."

Margaret says, "Of course, the plan is to have some art whether it's wall art, pottery, or sculpture just on loan for exhibits."

"That sounds great! We will be back in touch with you in about two weeks to make arrangements for our next visit."

Margaret says, "That sounds wonderful. I look forward to hearing from you."

CHAPTER 9

Henry is in his office, counting his money in his head, and all the things he can do with this money. Mr. Ameer Amjad had said he wanted to meet him on Tuesday of this week at the hunt club, so he can see what changes he might like to do and to sign the contract. He plans to bring some of his friends from other countries to enjoy a good hunt. Henry thinks anything that will make Mr. Amjad happy will just mean more money for him.

Back in Atlanta, in their suite, Mr. Sommeren and Mr. Amjad are having their lunch, talking over their good fortune and making plans as to what they need to make this great opportunity work in their favor. It has only been a little over six months since the September 11, 2001, attack, and they believe this is the best time for another. Their thoughts are that the American people would not expect another attack this close. And since this place, Mirror Lake, North Carolina, is on the east coast, it makes it the ideal place to set up and plan another attack on Washington.

The hunt club, being secluded like it is, makes a perfect cover for training, planning, and storing whatever they need to make this work. And the resort is a perfect way to bring in some of the people needed to pull this off, plus the gallery gives them some legitimacy.

After going to look over the hunt club and possibly getting help from some locals for work needed—which in itself makes them laugh—and getting it ready to bring in their comrades, Mr. Sommeren and Mr. Amjad will go back to Turkey to arrange a way to get anything else they need to make this work. Of course, a lot of the weapons needed have already been obtained from within the states, just waiting to be delivered to the hunt club once ready. And most of the soldiers are coming from sleeper cells within the United States. Once again, they feel that Allah has truly blessed them.

Henry calls Gordon to let him know he is meeting Mr. Amjad at the hunt club and wants to know if Gordon wants to go with him. After all, they're in this together, and Gordon hasn't met Mr. Amjad yet. Gordon agrees this is a good time for him to meet this Mr. Ameer Amjad and see what his plans are for the hunt club. It will not take more than four hours of his day, and he can be back at the bar for the evening crowd.

The meeting with Mr. Amjad didn't take as long as Henry and Gordon thought it would once they had signed the contract. Henry had taken the plat for the land, which showed all of the entrances and exits to the property and the surrounding roads in and out, as well as the blueprints of all the buildings. This allows Mr. Amjad to look over and hire someone to do any work he deems necessary, and Henry had already given him keys to everything. There is already running water and electricity on the property, and Henry has already had it turned on.

Mr. Amjad thanks Henry and lets him know he will be in touch to inform him of any changes he might make. Of course, Mr. Amjad states he will pay for any changes, and they will not come out of the money for the lease. This makes Henry very happy because he knows that will just benefit him even more. They say their goodbyes, and Henry and Gordon head back to Mirror Lake.

CHAPTER 10

Margaret picks up her phone and gives Helen a call. She says, "Hi, sis," as Helen answers.

"Hi right back at you," replies Helen.

Margaret continues to tell her about her conversation with Mr. Sommeren, and that they're willing to wait the time needed for Helen to get the gallery up and running. Margaret also says, "They want to bring art exhibits for display, as well as art to sell. I thought this was great because it draws all kinds of people into the gallery."

Helen, in reply, says, "That's great. Yes, I want this to be somewhat of a high-end gallery, and I believe we can pull it off with our local artist combined with a flare of Mideastern culture. Thanks for the great news. I need to get busy and get this place in shape."

As they say their goodbyes, Helen says to Margaret, "Thank you so much for being such a great sister. I really need this. Love you."

Margaret says, "Well, what's not to love. Love you right back. See you soon."

Helen heads back over to the old general store to meet with Billy Bob and go over what she needs from him and to show him what she's picked out online to order in the way of cabinets and lighting. She and Billy Bob go over everything, and he tells her this will not be hard to do. He says, "I'll have my guys here tomorrow to get started. We will first inspect the building, which, by the way, looks in good shape given the age. We will make sure the electricity is up to code, and now that I have your plans, I'll make sure you have all the outlets you need for the lighting and any other possible needs. We will then work on redoing the hardwood floors, and by then, you should have your cabinets and lights in and ready to install."

Helen says, "That's great. I've a rather short deadline to meet." She thanks Billy Bob for meeting her and lets him know she is very appreciative of his time. Once she's finished with Billy Bob, she goes ahead and places the order for items she needs.

Helen realizes she is hungry and makes her way to a little café that serves country cooking. When she enters the café, she sees Denton Gage, the new sheriff, sitting at a table by himself. Helen feels a little tingle and decides to walk over and say hello. Denton looks up just as Helen approaches and says, "Good afternoon, Helen, it's nice to see you."

Helen replies, "Thank you. It's nice to see you too. I didn't mean to interrupt your lunch, but I wanted to say hello to make sure you feel welcome in our little town."

Denton says, "Would you like to join me? That's if you are staying to eat!"

Helen says, "Well, I had planned on just picking up something. But if you don't mind the company, then, yes, I would love to join you." Helen sits, and the waitress comes over to take her order. She and Denton make small talk for a while. Helen tells Denton about the old general store and that a local contractor by the name of Billy Bob is going to do the renovations. Denton makes a comment, just like a Yankee, about the very southern name Billy Bob while Helen laughs. Denton again notices her smile and really likes her laugh.

As they finish their meal and prepare to leave, Denton says how nice it was to have company while eating. He makes the comment that he misses that. Helen understands where he is coming from even though she eats at home with her mother; most of the time, it isn't the same. It's nice to have someone to share your thoughts and plans with. Denton says, "I hope you don't think me to forward, but would you like to have dinner some time? It would really be nice to have someone to talk with while I eat, and you seem to be easy to talk with, and I haven't gotten acquainted with many of the townspeople yet."

Helen says, "That would be nice." Helen pulls out a piece of paper and writes her cell number on it and gives it to Denton.

He smiles and says, "Talk with you soon. Have a good day."

Helen just nods and smiles and says, "Same to you."

As Helen is headed back to her mother's, she can't help but think of Denton. He is a very handsome man in a rugged sort of way. Again, Helen feels that little tingle while thinking of Denton.

CHAPTER 11

Mr. Sommeren joins Mr. Amjad at the hunt club after Henry and Gordon have left. They go over the plat and the building plans, looking for ways to make this property even more secure. They would not want anyone to accidently wonder onto the property once they have their people in place. They're happy to find that the fencing around the property is six feet high. That's good, but they plan to electrify it and put sensors around the perimeters to help with the security. The buildings are fine the way they are—so really very little to be done. That's good. Their people can do all the work themselves, therefore, no outsiders necessary, less risk for anyone to become suspicious.

Mr. Amjad tells Mr. Sommeren that he can start contacting their people here in the states and have them start moving in this direction. Their plan is to have some of these people come to the resort on vacation and then come to the hunt club for training and planning. Mr. Amjad is going back to Turkey to meet with others that will be coming over to the resort, as well as to the hunt club as though for hunting, and of course, he's to arrange for some artwork along with some sculptures to be delivered for the gallery. They both agree that everything is going so smooth, and that they're ahead of schedule, which means that they may even move their attack date up. Their original plan was to attack on September 11—what better date for symbolism to remind the American people that they're not invincible. But, of course, they don't want to get ahead of themselves that would open them up to mistakes. They still have a lot to work out as far as the actual attack is concerned. They know that their target is Washington DC but not sure where. They want to make the biggest statement and most casualties as possible.

Mr. Amjad tells Mr. Sommeren to first get a number of their men here to do this bit of work and secure the area, then start with the others coming to the resort and possibly directly to the hunt club.

Mr. Sommeren first contacts the individuals they purchased the weapons from and gives them the directions to the hunt club and tells them to begin their journey. He lets them know that there would be someone on site to greet and show them where to store the merchandise. Then Mr. Sommeren leaves Atlanta headed to the Midwest to contact a number of the sleeper cells to start the migration of their people to Mirror Lake, North Carolina. Mr. Amjad leaves Atlanta, heads back to Istanbul to arrange for the art and sculpture to be shipped to Mirror Lake for the gallery.

CHAPTER 12

It has been just a little over three weeks since Margaret spoke with Mr. Sommeren, regarding their investment in the gallery. She is beginning to get a little worried because she hasn't heard from them. She keeps telling herself: no news is good news. She picks up her phone and gives Helen a call to see where the renovation stand and the art that's going into the gallery from the local artist. Helen answers and says, "Hi, sis, I bet I know why you're calling. You want to know where things stand."

Margaret says, "Yes, I'm sorry, just a little antsy because I haven't heard anything from Mr. Sommeren."

Helen says, "Quit worrying. It's all coming together, so if we get nothing from these guys, it will be all right. I'm tired of worrying, and you are really going to love the stuff I've already gotten. It's amazing."

Margaret says, "No, you are the one that's amazing. You have so much riding on this, I just don't want to disappoint you."

"You could never disappointment me, and I'm beginning to think that all of this local talent is going to go over even bigger than anything that could come from the Middle East. Besides, Denton says everything looks great."

Margaret, with a little smile, says, "Oh really, so Denton says it's great. I know we haven't talked a lot lately, but okay, what is going on up there? You seem to be keeping me in the dark."

Helen laughs. "No, it isn't like that. We have just had dinner a couple of times, and Denton comes by the gallery just about every day, so he does not mind giving me his opinion."

Margaret says, "Okay, if you say so. I think I'll come up there this weekend and see what things look like for myself, and just maybe, I'll hear something before then."

Helen just says, "Let me know when to expect you."

Helen smiles to herself about the comments from Margaret regarding Denton. She's really enjoyed their dinners, and even more the times he just drops by to talk with her, and he seems to really love what she's done with the gallery, which makes her feel really good about things.

*****

Mr. Sommeren is at the hunt club and has been most of the last two weeks. Everything is coming together just fine. All of the security is in place, and the weapons that they have already obtained are there and so are most of the people that they need to keep the place secure and to start the planning. He gives Mr. Amjad a call to see where he stands with the artwork and the rest of their funding for this attack and the other people they're expecting. He needs to give Margaret O'Keefe a call before she starts to worry. Mr. Amjad lets him know that everything is a go; he has the art ready to ship, and that he will be sending the info and instruction for the shipment to Mr. Sommeren to pass on to Ms. O'Keefe.

The shipment should be reaching Atlanta within the next week. And as far as everything else, Mr. Amjad tells Mr. Sommeren, "I'll be in Atlanta within the next two days and will fill you in on everything else then?"

Mr. Sommeren gives Margaret a call to let her know the status of things. Margaret answers her phone.

"Hello, Margaret, Mr. Sommeren here. I'm sorry it has been so long since we spoke last, but I come bearing good news. Mr. Amjad and I both agree that the art and antiquities gallery is the direction in which we want to go, even though we haven't yet seen it. We both are excited about displaying and possibly selling some of our countries artwork, hoping to share a little piece of our culture."

Margaret is so excited; she is at a loss for words.

Mr. Sommeren says, "Margaret, are you there? Can you hear me?"

Margaret coughs a little and says, "Oh yes, sir, sorry you just took me by surprise. I was not expecting your response this soon. But don't misunderstand, I'm delighted in your decision. I don't believe you'll be disappointed. The gallery is ready, and I believe within the next week will be ready for their open house, which I hope you and Mr. Amjad will be able to attend. Have you made any arrangements for any artwork for the gallery as of yet?"

Mr. Sommeren replies, "Yes, it should reach Atlanta in about a week."

"That's wonderful news. I'll let Mrs. Colman know, and hopefully we'll be able to incorporate it into the displays in time for the open house."

Mr. Sommeren says, "That would be wonderful. Mr. Amjad should be back in the country by then, and we both would be able to attend the open house. I'll be in touch with you in a few days with instructions on when to expect the shipment."

Margaret says, "I'll look forward to hearing back from you."

CHAPTER 13

Helen is at the gallery, making her last inspection before saying good-bye to Billy Bob, who has done an outstanding job on the renovations and in record time. She already has a back room full of items to display and sale from local artist. She and Billy Bob are just wrapping up when in walks Denton. Helen hands Billy Bob his final payment and again tells him what a wonderful job he's done and how proud she is of the gallery. It's everything she had hoped it would be. Now the fun part starts, setting everything up and getting ready for the open house.

Once Billy Bob had gone, Denton, while looking around again, tells Helen how great everything looks. Helen says, "Just wait until you see all the items I have to display. I'm totally overwhelmed with all of the local talent, and how willing everyone is to have their art displayed and sold in my little gallery?"

Denton ask, "When do you plan to open and are you having an open house?"

Helen, in response, says, "I'm thinking Saturday, May 18, and plan on combining the grand opening with the open house. What do you think?"

Denton says, "Why not? That sounds like a solid plan to me." Denton asks Helen to dinner that evening, so he can hear more about her plans. Helen says that sounds good to her. Denton asks if she is okay with coming to his place; he would like to cook dinner for her. Helen says yes, and they set a time for 7:00 p.m.

As Denton is saying goodbye to Helen, her phone rings. As she answers, it's Margaret. "Helen, I'm so glad I was able to reach you. I've some great news."

Helen says, "Hold on just a minute." Helen then turns and says goodbye and see you later this evening to Denton. Helen says, "Okay, I'm back, so what is this good news you have?"

Margaret replies, "I've just got off the phone with Mr. Sommeren, and they're a go as far as the gallery is concerned and sight unseen."

Helen says, "That's great news! So do we have any information on what they plan as far as art goes."

Margaret replies, "Yes, a shipment of art should be in Atlanta within a week. I'll have more on what is in this shipment in a day or two. Do you think you are ready for this shipment?"

Helen says, "Yes, I'm starting today, putting out my other displays. Are you still planning to come up this weekend?"

"Yes, I want to see the gallery and also talk about the open house. Do you have a plan for the open house yet?"

"Yes, I was thinking Saturday the eighteenth for actually the whole shebang, grand opening and open house? What do you think?"

"Sounds like a great plan, and that will give me time to make the arrangements for Mr. Sommeren and Mr. Amjad at the resort. They both plan to be there for the opening."

Helen drives out to Denton's modest three-bedrooms-and-two-baths log cabin. She knows the place; it has been there for years just outside of the city limits back in the woods. It really suits him, she thinks. Denton was on the back porch, attending to the steaks he was grilling for them. He had also thrown on the grill some corn on the cob and baked them each a potato—the kind of meal he really goes for. He hopes Helen enjoys this kind of meal. He hears a noise and turns to see Helen standing at his back door. He says, "Hello, glad to see you could find the place."

Helen replies, "I knocked, but you didn't answer. The door was open, so I came on in. And this old place, I know it like the back of my hand. When I was a little girl, I use to come out here and walk down to the lake and go fishing. One of my best friends used to live here. I believe it has been updated quite a bit since then. It really looks good. Something sure smells good. I hope it's about ready. I'm starving."

Denton likes what he hears as he says, "Good. It's ready to put on the table. Now we have a choice, we can eat out here on the porch or inside. What's your pleasure?"

Helen answers, "Let's eat on the porch. It's such a nice evening." Helen sets the table while Denton takes up the food, and they set at the table on his back porch.

As they eat, Denton starts asking her about the gallery. He knows about the local art but hasn't heard much about any other items she is planning to use. Denton says, "I know you have quite a bit of local art, sculpture, and even some metal artwork, but you have told me very little about what Margaret has arranged."

Helen says, "Well, you know she is a finical advisor in Atlanta, and she has these new clients who seem to be extremely interested in my little gallery. They have already arranged a shipment of art that will arrive in Atlanta in about a week. They were so excited about the gallery they were willing to invest without even seeing it. I was surprised but pleased. It will give my little gallery just a bit of flare, don't you think?"

Denton can't help but think that it seems a little odd to him, but you never know about rich people no matter where they're from. Then Denton asks, "Where are these investor's from?"

Helen says, "Not totally sure, just somewhere in the Middle East, I think."

Denton replies, "That's great! It's always good to have verity, don't you think?"

Helen agrees, and they continue to enjoy their evening.

CHAPTER 14

Saturday, May 4, Margaret drives up to Mirror Lake; she arrives at her mother's, Mildred's, home about 1:00 p.m. Helen is just finishing up getting ready to head into town. She had agreed to meet Denton for lunch at their favorite little café, the one that serves country cooking. Margaret walks into Helen's bedroom and says, "So why are you dressing up so much?"

Helen stutters in surprise of the question and says, "I'm not dressed up, and it isn't a crime to want to look nice."

Margaret says with a little laugh, "So who or why are you looking nice for? Mother has been keeping me up-to-date about your evenings out."

"Oh, she has, has she? So exactly what has she been telling you?"

Margaret, in reply, says, "That you have had dinner with Denton Gage on numerous occasions, and that the last one was at his home where he cooked you dinner. What do you have to say for yourself?"

Helen laughs. "You just have to make something out of nothing, don't you? He is just a friend, and I just happen to enjoy his company. He's really been helpful with everything even if it's just through listening and encouragement."

"Then I'm glad that he is your friend, and it's nice to see you smiling so much again."

Helen tells Margaret on their way out that they're meeting Denton at the little café, Maddie's Country Cooking on Main Street. Margaret says, "Well, now we are moving into two meals a day, isn't that cozy."

When they get to Maddie's café, Denton is already there waiting for them. He waves at them as they walk into the café. Margaret greets Denton with hello and a smile as she and Helen sit with him at the table. They all order their food, then Denton says, "Margaret, I hope you had a good drive up this morning?"

Margaret replies, "Yes, I did. It was very uneventful. Thank you for asking."

Denton asks, "I assume you are here to see the gallery and help Helen with final touches, getting ready for the open house? It really is coming together very well."

Margaret replies, "Yes, I am, and I'm excited about all of it! Helen has been keeping me informed on her progress and sounds like she really does not need my help, but I just couldn't wait to see how it has turned out. Helen told me that you have been very helpful with the gallery."

Helen says to Denton, "Margaret has good news as well, and that is her clients from the Middle East are shipping some art to Atlanta as we speak. It looks like it will be here in time for the open house."

Denton says, "That sounds nice. Do you know what kind of art they're shipping? Like actual wall art, sculptures, or whatever?"

Margaret says, "No, I thought I would have a list of the inventory by now but didn't receive it before I left Atlanta."

Helen says, "That's a shame. I would love to know what to expect, so I could arrange what I already have accordingly to allow proper space for their art."

Margaret says, "I know, sis, sorry. But as soon as I get it, I'll fax or email it to you."

"That's fine, we will work around whatever we have to, and I believe this grand opening will be spectacular, and it couldn't come at a better time of the year. Things really get hopping around here in late spring and earlier summer with all of the tourist pouring into town."

Denton says, "I certainly know one person who is especially happy with the idea of the gallery bringing more attention to Mirror Lake." Before Denton could say who, he was thinking about all three of them said in unison, "Mayor Henry Mason," and they all laughed.

Helen says, "I almost forgot, Margaret, I had Billy Bob replace the front doors to the gallery. You know how they were old wood doors and really were not in the best of shape. I had him replace them with all glass doors, and they're spectacular. Aren't they, Denton?"

Denton says, "Yes, they are. It really gives a very high-end design to the gallery."

CHAPTER 15

Mr. Amjad has arrived back in Atlanta and meets up with Mr. Sommeren, so they can go over everything else needed for this attack. Mr. Sommeren fills Mr. Amjad in on all they have accomplished. Everything at the hunt club is ready; they're just waiting for everyone else to get there so they can start planning and training. Mr. Amjad is very pleased to hear this and is excited about making plans of what their actual target will be in Washington. Again, they discuss their time line, and if they think there is a possibility to move the attack up. Mr. Amjad says to Mr. Sommeren, "I'm not sure I want to move the date up even if we are ready before September 11. I still like the symbolism of using September 11. I think it can do just about as much damage as the destruction of property and of persons."

Mr. Sommeren says, "I understand, but if we are ready ahead of time and don't strike, it makes us more vulnerable to being discovered."

Mr. Amjad says, "Yes, I guess you are right. We will just have to wait and see how things come together."

*****

Henry and Gordon sit at the bar in the G&G Bar and Grill on Saturday, May 4, talking about Mr. Amjad and the hunt club. Gordon asks, "Have you talked with Mr. Amjad since he signed the contract and paid for the first year?"

Henry replies, "No, I haven't heard a word from him. I thought about giving him a call but really have no reason to call him. I'm curious as to how things are going at the hunt club. As far as I know, he never hired anyone locally to do any work like he mentioned he was going to do. I would love to see what he's done if anything and what is going on up there. I haven't heard of anyone making travel arrangements to get there. But this Mr. Amjad is a very private man, and I get the feeling he isn't interested in having anything to do with the locals."

Gordon says, "Well, that's not necessarily a bad thing, is it? I mean if he is bringing people from other parts of the country, or world it just means more money for the resort and Mirror Lake, right?"

Henry replies, "Yeah, I guess so, I just would really like to see what is going on up there, and also if there is going to be publicity. I would like to be a part of that. It would look good for me as mayor of Mirror Lake."

Gordon says, "Well, I guess you are right about that but not much you can do about it, is there?"

Henry replies, "I don't know. I'm just thinking on it. Maybe I'll find a good reason to go up there and take a look around, then maybe get invited to join them at least in one hunt."

Gordon says, "Are you sure about that? It might not be a good idea. You don't want to upset the applecart. I mean you know we want them to take that second-year option on the lease. That's too much money to risk losing, don't you think?"

"Yeah, but I sure want to be a part of any publicity if it's really big. Maybe I'll have to hire someone to just go up there and look around. They can always go up as though they're hunting in the area, you know, to see what they can see."

Gordon says, "I might know someone we can get. Let me do some checking, and I'll let you know. It will not cost much a good steak and some beer. I'll let you know in a few days, and we will talk about when you want this done.

CHAPTER 16

Later in the week, Helen is at the gallery, working on putting things together. She's heard from Margaret and is expecting the shipment from Mr. Sommeren by Saturday, May 11, or at least by Monday, May 13. She is working real hard to get things sorted and figuring out how she wants them displayed. It isn't easy since she does not have the list of items from the Middle East. Margaret is supposed to be getting that to her by tomorrow, and that will at least help.

Denton has been coming by every day, supposedly checking on her progress, but in all actuality, it's just to see Helen. Truth be known, Helen is just as happy to see Denton no matter what the reason. They really seem to get along very well. They have so much in common, and it's nice that they both don't mind taking it slow. Who knows it might never go any further than the friendship they have now, and that's okay with Helen if it doesn't.

Henry Mason drops by the gallery while Helen is working, just to see how it looks. Henry says to Helen, "Boy, everything is really looking great…so high-end. If this does not make a difference with the tourist crowd, I don't know what will. I love the art from the locals, but I thought you were bringing in some pieces from outside?"

Helen, in reply, says, "I am. There is a shipment expected to arrive in just a few days. It's art that's coming from the Middle East."

"Oh really, I didn't know that you had those kinds of contacts. What kind of art?"

"I'm not sure yet what will be in this shipment. I'll be getting an inventory list by tomorrow. Margaret has arranged this for me. It's coming from some new clients of hers. They were looking for some investments and liked the idea of my gallery. They actually haven't invested in the gallery itself, but I'll get a percentage of any sales that we make. Also, they're bringing some items just for display to help promote their culture."

"Oh, what part of the Middle East are they from?"

"I think it's Turkey, but I haven't actually met them yet. They plan on being here for the grand opening."

Henry says, "That's great, and have you set a date for this grand opening?"

"Yes, I have. If all goes well, and it should, I plan for it to be on Saturday, May 18."

"Well, that's a fine thing. When were you planning to tell me about this grand opening?"

Helen says, "As soon as I was sure and had everything in place. I saw no reason to start rumors before I had everything ready."

Henry responds, "Well, I think, being mayor after all, you should keep me informed on these things. It affects the whole town."

Helen stifles a little laugh and says, "Well, I know how important it is to the town, but again, I didn't want to jump the gun. Don't worry, Henry, it will all fall into place and will be a very nice grand opening. I promise it will make you and everyone on the board of the chamber of commerce proud."

As Henry is walking out of the gallery in a bit of huff, Denton is coming in. Denton says, "Hello, mayor, hope you are having a good day."

Henry really does not answer, just walks right past Denton in a hurry. Denton looks at Helen and says, "What's his problem?"

Helen laughs. "Oh, he has his shorts in wad because I haven't said anything to him about the grand opening."

Denton says, "Really what difference does that make?"

"Well, he thinks since he is mayor, he should be informed of everything that's happening in our little town of Mirror Lake. He will get over it eventually."

Denton replies, "I'm sure he will, but he might never let you forget it."

They both just laugh, then Denton asks, "How about lunch?"

Helen says, "That sounds great."

They head out to their favorite little café, Maddie's.

CHAPTER 17

Margaret is wondering why she hasn't received the list of inventory from Mr. Sommeren for the shipment that's arriving today in Atlanta and then will head out tomorrow for Mirror Lake. Since she hasn't heard anything more from Mr. Sommeren, she decides to give him a call.

Mr. Sommeren's phone rings, and he sees its Margaret. He wonders why she is calling. He picks up and says, "Hello, Margaret, how can I help you? I hope there hasn't been a problem with our shipment."

Margaret says, "No, but I never received the inventory list for the shipment."

Mr. Sommeren is thinking. "Was I supposed to give a list of inventory?" He just does not remember this at all.

Since there was a bit of silence on his end, Margaret continuous, "You were going to send me a list of the inventory, so I could get it to Mrs. Coleman to help her with preparing the design for the gallery opening."

This jogged Mr. Sommeren's memory as he says, "Oh yes, I'm so sorry. I've just been so busy it slipped my mind. I'll fax it right over. Please except my apologies."

Margaret replies, "That's quiet all right. I understand. There is just not much time left before the grand opening of the gallery, and the list will help tremendously in getting ready for the opening."

Mr. Sommeren says, "Do you have a date for the opening?"

Margaret replies, "Yes, Mrs. Coleman plans for the grand opening to be on Saturday, May 18. I should have all of the details in just a few days and will get it right to you along with your written invitation."

Mr. Sommeren says, "That will be great, and that inventory list should be coming over any minute now."

"Yes, I have it, and thank you for your prompt response."

Margaret gives Helen a call to let her know she is faxing over the list of inventory as she speaks. Helen is happy to get it. This will help tremendously with the final placement of all the artwork she has, and then she can focus on the invitations. After all, she isn't going to have much time to get the invitations out and the advertisements done to give enough time before the opening. She really wants this to go over well, not just for herself but for the town as well. Helen is very proud of her little town and really wants to see it do well. Even if she isn't overly found of Henry Mason, their mayor, Mirror Lake is home, and the people of Mirror Lake are family. Also she realizes she wants Denton Gage to be happy; he chose Mirror Lake as his new home.

Helen's phone rings, and it's Denton. He says, "I know you are real busy, but how about dinner tonight?"

Helen responds, "You are right. I'm really busy, but a girl has to eat. What are you thinking about?"

Denton says, "Don't know, just would enjoy your company for dinner. Do you have any ideas?"

"Well, how does Chinese sound? You could pick it up and bring it over to the gallery, and we could eat here, and maybe I could persuade you to help me move somethings around? I have the inventory list for the new items coming in from the Middle East, so I think I can get the layout I want before it actually arrives."

Denton replies, "That sounds good to me. What would you like to eat from the Chinese place?"

"I know I'll be hungry by then so surprise me and then be prepared to do some heavy lifting."

Denton says, "Okay, I'll see you around six."

CHAPTER 18

It's about 10:00 p.m. on Wednesday, May 8, and Henry is sitting at the bar in the G&G Bar and Grill, talking with Gordon. Henry asks Gordon, "Have you found someone that knows the area where the hunt club is to snoop around yet?"

Gordon says, "I've several guys lined up, but I'm thinking we only need two boys to do the job. Any more than that and they might get a little too ambitious and do something stupid."

"I believe you are right in your thinking on that. It's one thing to pay someone to do this kind of thing for us, but you know some of these guys get a little greedy."

"That's for sure, and the two I'm thinking about will not cost much at all, a little cash and a lot of beer."

"Are you sure they can pull this off without giving us away?"

Gordon says, "Sure, how hard can it be just two guys hunting and stumbling into the area? And just maybe they can talk to a few of the people there and maybe get invited in so they can even have a better look around."

"As long as you think they can handle it, I'll leave it in your hands."

"Okay, then I'll arrange for them to do this in the next few days."

*****

Earlier in the evening, Denton picks up the Chinese food and heads over to the gallery. When he walks in, Helen is up on a ladder, trying to measure an area for a piece of wall art. He immediately puts the food down and rushes over to her just as she is about to topple over. Denton catches her before she can fall.

46

Helen says, "Oh my god, I didn't realize I was reaching so far. Thanks."

Denton responds, "You must be more careful, or you'll not be around to open this gallery. What are you trying to do?"

"I need some measurements to make sure this piece fits where I want it to go. I thought I could do this without any help, but I guess that was not a smart idea."

"No, it wasn't. It's one thing to climb on a ladder, but you never do it while along."

"I promise I won't try that again. I smell something good, and I just realized I'm starving."

"Then let's eat, and then I'll tackle anything you need me to do."

Helen thinks, *I'm so glad he is around. It's not only pleasant but also helpful.*

*****

The next day, Gordon contacts the two guys. He plans to send on their little fishing expedition for information about what is going on at the hunt club. He's chosen two boys around the age of twenty-two. Their names are Chuck Anderson and Donald Dawson. They both have a reputation of being a little on the slow side and will do anything just about for beer.

Gordon gives them the area he wants them to look at and tells them that they must be careful and not to mention his name nor Henry's. They just need to appear that they were hunting and just stumbled upon the hunt club, also to act as though they know nothing about the club, or that it was even there. He wants them to look around and see what they can see, and if by chance they get invited in, they just make note of anything they think might have changed or take some pictures with their phones—but again makes sure they don't mention Gordon or Henry or even Mirror Lake. The two boys assure Gordon they can handle this, and they would head out on Tuesday the fourteenth or Wednesday the fifteenth and be back within a few days. Gordon says that it sounds great.

CHAPTER 19

It's Monday, May 13, and Helen is at the gallery, awaiting the shipment that should be there any minute. She is so excited she can't wait to see what these things look like. She already has a good idea of how and what pieces she wants to start with. It will not be possible to put them all out. But from the inventory list, she's picked the pieces she believes that Mr. Sommeren and Mr. Ameer Amjad would want to see out on opening night, and then as the weeks go on and depending on how the sales go then, more pieces will come out and hopefully will sell.

This part is real important to her being able to maintain the gallery. Of course, the local art should move fast as well. Some of these pieces are really beautiful. Helen has already been to the local printer and has given the order for the invitations that she and Margaret worked up for the grand opening. It isn't that many. They're mostly for what they consider the elite of Mirror Lake and a few others. Of course, the grand opening will be open to the public. This is what the advertisements were for. Helen really hopes to see a lot of people there. Of course, this is the start of their busy season for the resort, so there should be a lot of tourist in town. So this should help the gallery and also the other shops in town. It should be big for all of Mirror Lake.

Margaret calls Helen, "How goes it? Has the shipment arrived?"

Helen responds, "No, not yet, but should be here any minute, and I can't wait. I want to finish up getting the gallery ready for the opening on Saturday, so I can then focus on the food. I've done very little in that area. Of course, it's just going to be finger foods, and I'm thinking I need to have a wine bar. What do you think?"

Margaret responds, "For sure, it needs to be wine and cheese, and of course, you can throw in a few other things to eat, but wine and cheese just says elegance."

Helen says, "I believe you are right, and I should be able to do this in a day."

"You also need to think about what you are going to wear."

Helen replies, "I know, but I don't have a thing that will work for this, and I'm not sure that any of the boutiques in town would have anything that would work either."

Margaret says, "No worries, I'll pick up a couple of things and bring them up. I plan to be there on Thursday night. That way I can help with any last-minute things you need help with. Is Denton going to escort you to the grand opening?"

Helen says, "No, why would he? I don't need an escort. I'm sure he is going to be there, and that's good enough."

Margaret giggles. "You do protest too much, I think. Could it be you like him just a little?"

Helen says, "Of course, I like him as a friend, and he's been a lot of help to me with getting the gallery ready but don't try to make a mountain out of a molehill."

Margaret just laughs. She loves picking on her sister, but she is also glad to see Helen happy and smiling a lot more; she deserves it.

*****

Chuck and Donald are on their little excursion to the upper norther section of the mountains of North Carolina, and they have no clue as to what they're walking into. They're not far from the hunt club when all of a sudden, several men appear out of nowhere. They're dressed in camouflage and have automatic weapons. Chuck and Donald don't know what to think. Their first thoughts are to run but realize that would be stupid. The men don't say anything, just push them in the direction of the hunt club. Of course, the men have already taken their rifles from them and also their backpacks. There is nothing for them to do but to go where the men want them to go.

Once inside the hunt club, they're locked in a building alone. Chuck says to Donald, "What have we got ourselves into?"

Donald says, "This is like no hunt club I've ever seen."

Mr. Sommeren is still in Atlanta with Mr. Amjad when he gets a call from the hunt club. Mr. Sommeren answers his phone and just listens. Then he looks at Mr. Amjad and says, "We have a problem."

Mr. Amjad responds, "What kind of problem?"

"There are two young men that have been taken into the camp and locked up. They appear to be hunters and just stumbled on to the camp. They want to know what to do with them. The problem is, they took them at gunpoint, and now they have seen the camp."

Mr. Amjad replies, "Well, they leave us with little option, don't they? We must get rid of them in a way they will never be found. But first, we need to know if anyone knows where they are."

Mr. Sommeren just nods; he understands what Mr. Amjad is saying. He goes back to the phone and gives instructions on what to do with the two intruders. Hopefully this will not come back to them later before they can complete their attack. The men at the camp start questing Chuck and Donald about where they come from and who knows where they are. Of course, they swear they were just out hunting, and that no one knows where they are. They get knock around a bit, and they're really scared, but they're trying to do what Gordon ask them to and not let on that they were sent by him.

But all of a sudden Chuck thinks he sees an opportunity to get away, so he bolts for the door and is shot in the back by one of the men in the room, and Donald just breaks down and starts crying. He tells them that they were sent by someone from Mirror Lake, but he does not give a name up. They beat him more, and before they realize it, they have beaten him to death. They take both bodies to the upper northeast corner of the camp and douse them with gasoline and set them on fire, then cover over the ashes. This should take care of everything.

CHAPTER 20

It's Thursday night, May 16, and Margaret has arrived at her mother's. She's brought several gowns for Helen to try for the gallery opening. Helen tries on both; one is royal blue and is strapless, and the other is a beautiful emerald green, and it's backless. They both fit like a glove, but Margaret says, "Oh, Helen, the green one is the one. You look unbelievable. You'll certainly be the bell of the ball, and Denton will go crazy."

Helen just rolls her eyes and says, "Okay, you are exaggerating as you always do, but I have to say I love this one, and green is my favorite color after all. So the green one it is. What are you planning to wear?"

Margaret says, "I've a lovely little silver number I picked up for me. It really shows off my legs."

Helen just laughs and thinks they really are a pair, but they do know how to have fun no matter how old they get. She hopes that never changes.

It's now 6:00 p.m., Saturday, May the 18, and Helen and Margaret are headed out to the gallery. Margaret, earlier that morning, made sure that Mr. Sommeren and Mr. Amjad had arrived and were set with everything they needed. The grand opening is scheduled for 7:30 p.m. Helen wants to be there early enough to make sure everything is in place. Of course, she and Margaret spent the morning there with the caterers, making sure everything was set up and ready for the food to arrive. Margaret said everything was really beautiful, and she noticed that Helen had changed out the front doors for all beveled glass with overhead lighting, which makes the gallery even more beautiful. She couldn't help but think that this venture was going to be great.

*****

Henry and Gordon were at the G&G Bar and Grill, talking and having a last-minute drink before heading out to the gallery. Henry says to Gordon, "Have you heard anything from the two boys you sent out to check on the hunt club?"

Gordon responds, "No, but I'm not worried. They tend to forget time. They're in the woods where they seem to stay a lot, and I'm sure they're drinking, but they should be back no later than Monday. I'll keep you informed. We better head on over to the gallery, don't you think? You want to be one of the first ones there, correct?"

"Yeah, I guess you are right. Let's head out."

They get to the gallery about 7:15 p.m. and greet Helen and Margaret, and of course, Denton arrives about the same time. They all nod and say their hellos. Denton is smiling at Helen, and looking her up and down, he steps over to her and leans into her ear and says, "You are stunning."

Helen looks up into his eyes and just smiles.

Denton says, "I know you have to greet people as they come in, so I'll get out of your way and just head over to the bar and get a glass of wine. We can talk later."

Helen says, "Thanks. After the event is over, we will have time then."

Denton looks at her and says, "I certainly hope so."

When Mr. Sommeren and Mr. Amjad arrive, Margaret and Helen both are there to greet them. Margaret introduces them, "Mr. J. Sommeren and Mr. Ameer Amjad, I would like you to meet Mrs. Coleman, the curator and owner of the gallery."

Helen holds out her hand to both men, and they both shake her hand, and Mr. Sommeren says, "What a pleasure it is to meet you and see the gallery. It's everything we have heard it would be."

Mr. Amjad just nods in agreement; he is a man of few words.

Helen says, "Please take your time and let Margaret show you around and enjoy a glass of wine. I think you'll be happy with the items I've chosen from your generous inventory and the way they have been displayed. But, of course, I want to hear your thoughts on everything. Please enjoy while I greet my other guest."

Margaret encourages them to follow her, and they walk away. Helen stays close to the door, so she can great others still coming in. She will walk around a little later and answer any question anyone might have. Of course, she has a staff to help with this as well for anyone who is interested in buying.

Henry and Gordon have walked around and looked at everything and commented on how well Helen had done with the gallery and her displays. They're over at the bar with Denton when Henry notices Margaret with two men that are dress very similar to Mr. Ameer Amjad. When he looks a little closer, he realized it's Mr. Amjad. He punches Gordon in the side and says, "Look who is here."

Gordon stops talking with Denton and looks in Margaret's direction and sees Mr. Amjad. He says to Henry, "Did you invite him here?"

Henry says, "No, I didn't. I didn't think about it."

Gordon says, "So how did he find out about it?"

Denton is standing just listening to them and says, "Do you know those gentlemen?"

Henry says, "Yeah, kind of."

Denton says in return, "Actually what does kind of mean?"

Henry responds, "Well, we have done a little business with them on a lease for some property up in the northeast corner of the state."

Denton, in reply, says, "Is that so? What is their interest in leasing land in the North Carolina mountains?"

Henry says, "It belongs to my family, and once was a hunt club, and they're going to do some fox hunting with some of their acquaintance from other countries, and of course, some of their friends from the states."

Denton thinks that's a little strange to him; he will have to remember to get their names and info from Helen and do a little checking. Henry and Gordon never got a chance to speak with Mr.

Amjad before they left the gallery. Henry thinks he will contact Mr. Amjad tomorrow and use the fact that he was at the grand opening of the gallery as an excuse to talk with him. Maybe he can find out a little something about the hunt club.

The opening is over, and everyone has left including Margaret, who has headed back to her mother's. Helen and Denton are the only two left. Helen is getting ready to lock up. As she goes to turn out the lights, Denton takes her hand and pulls it up to his lips for a light kiss. He says softly, "You really amaze me. The grand opening couldn't have gone any better. And you were the most elegant and beautiful woman here." He puts his hand around her waist and pulls her close, and with his hand under her chin, he turns her face up to look in her eyes. Helen isn't quite sure what to do, but before she could think about it, Denton lowers his mouth to hers and kisses her softly. All she can do is kiss him back. This is the most intimate they have been, and Helen can't help but think it really feels good. Denton just looks at her and lets her go as she turns out the lights and locks the doors. Denton asks, "Would you like to come over to my place for a while?"

Helen says, "I better not. Margaret and mother is expecting me home. Denton, I really like you, and you have been more than wonderful through everything. But I believe we both have been through a lot in our lives, and maybe we still need to take things a little slow."

Denton, in reply, says, "I understand and agree. It's just this night, and the way you look really makes me feel good. Do you need a ride home?"

Helen, in reply, says, "Yes, I guess I do, I forgot Margaret and I came together, and she took the car when she left."

Denton says, "I'll be happy to make sure you get home safe, and it will give me an opportunity to kiss you again."

Helen looks up in his eyes and smiles.

CHAPTER 21

Margaret is waiting up when Helen walks into the house. Margaret says, "I was wondering if you were going to come home tonight" and smiles.

Helen says, "Well, of course, I was coming home. Where else would I go?"

Margaret just grins. "Well, I thought you might at least take a little detour. Why do you think I left earlier and took the car?"

Helen replies, "I didn't even think about that or the car until it was time for me to come home. Of course, Denton was nice enough to bring me home."

"So are you telling me nothing happen at all? He just gave you a ride home?"

Helen smiles and says nothing.

Margaret says again, "Okay, that smile tells me it was more than just a ride, so spill the beans. Or you'll not sleep all night, I'll make sure of that."

Helen laughs then says, "He kissed me, and I kissed him back. And, oh, Margaret, it was really nice. He told me I was amazing and beautiful then asks me to go home with him."

Margaret, in response, says, "Well, why didn't you go home with him? Are you crazy? I would have gone home with him in a heartbeat!"

Helen, in reply, says, "I'm not quite sure, but I really like him. It just seems like it hasn't been long enough for me to have feelings for someone else you know. I kind of feel like I'm not being true to Gus."

Margaret says, "You know that's not true. Gus would want you to go on with your life and be happy. Denton is a good man, and I'm sure it's not easy for him as well."

"I know. We have never really talked about this. We just dance around it and flirt. I'm not sure how to start that kind of conversation."

"Just be straight with him, and the rest will fall into place. You both come from a similar situation."

"I know we do, and I guess that's why it's so hard. I know how I feel, and I think I know about how he feels. It's just hard to put into words."

Margaret replies, "I know I can't say I totally understand because I've never been in your situation before, but I do know I would not let the possibility of a relationship with a man like Denton get away just because I was not sure what to say."

"I know you are right, and I promise I'll not give up on this, and even if it ends in just a good friendship, I'll be okay with that. Now can we go to bed? I'm really tired. We can talk about this more tomorrow."

Margaret laughs. "Yes, I guess you are right. See you in the morning. Sleep well."

"Thanks for being a great sister and being honest with me. Good night."

*****

Denton has made it home but can't seem to sleep because he can't stop thinking about Helen. He is conflicted about his feelings. He really loved his wife and misses her terribly, but he seems to have feelings for Helen Coleman as well. He is just not sure what to do with these feelings. He can't get a handle on how she feels. Like tonight, he is pretty sure what he would like to have happened if she would have come home with him, but since she didn't, he is having a hard time reading her. He thinks she likes him based on their relationship but not sure if it will go any further. He believes he wants it to. Just trying to get past the quilt, he feels. He decides he needs to think about something else, or he will never get to sleep. Then he remembers the conversation between Henry and Gordon, regarding the two gentlemen that were at the gallery with Margaret. He believes they're the ones Helen has talked about investing in the gallery. Then he remembers his little talk with Henry and Gordon about the two gentlemen, and he knows that come Monday morning, he needs to do a little checking into these two men. He can use that as an excuse to go to the gallery and see Helen. She should have their names or at least be able to get them from Margaret.

CHAPTER 22

Helen and Margaret spend the day with their mother, Mildred, on Sunday, May 19. They talked about old times and spoke with their other two sisters, Pat and Melonie, checking on their lives and families and letting them know how the grand opening went. Before Margaret leaves to go back to Atlanta, she asks Helen what she is going to do about Denton. Helen tells her she isn't sure but promises she will keep her informed. They say their goodbyes, and Margaret heads back to Atlanta.

Mr. Sommeren and Mr. Amjad are still at the resort in Mirror Lake; they're planning on staying just a few more days then heading up to the camp. Mr. Amjad asks Mr. Sommeren, "Has our little problem been taken care of?"

Mr. Sommeren replies, "Yes, it has but not to my satisfaction. They didn't get much information from the young men, just that they were sent by someone from Mirror Lake. They did dispose of the bodies in a way that should not be a problem."

"Well, not knowing who would have sent them is a real problem."

"Do you think it could be this Henry Mason fellow?"

Mr. Amjad says, "No, I don't think he is that smart, plus he is more concerned with the money than anything else, including what is going on at the camp."

Mr. Sommeren thinks about how much they have accomplished in just a short period of time; it makes him want to go ahead and change the date for the attack for earlier than September 11. He thinks that if they're not careful, someone will find out and interrupt their plans. But he knows that Mr. Amjad is set on using the September 11 date for the effect it will have, as well as the destruction.

Mr. Amjad says to Mr. Sommeren, "I know we have the weapons we need, but did they get the trucks and the decals needed to disguise the trucks for transport along with the men?"

Mr. Sommeren responds, "Yes, I believe we have everything we need, and we have gone over the plans and the place for the attack. We all agree that the National Mall of Washington DC, is the perfect target. It's centrally located in Washington, stretching over two miles from the Lincoln Memorial on the west end to the US capitol on the east end. There are thousands of people on any given day, visiting the mall. It's so close to the capitol. They will know that there is no place we can't reach."

*****

Henry calls Gordon on Monday morning to see if he's heard from Chuck and Donald. Gordon says no but let him do some checking, and he will get back to him. Gordon starts calling around to some of their drinking buddies, but no one has seen them since they left last Wednesday. He has to say the boys did well; they didn't tell any of their buddies what they were doing just that they were going to do a little hunting.

Gordon calls Henry, "No one has seen or heard from them since they left last Wednesday. They told everyone they were going hunting but didn't say where. That's a good thing, but we have no way of checking on them."

Henry says, "Don't they have cell phones?"

Gordon responds, "Don't you think I would have already checked that way? You know there is no service up there. At least not good, it's spotted at best."

Henry replies, "I know what kind of service there is up there, but what are we going to do if we don't hear from them?"

"We just give them a little more time. It's not like they were going to drive right up to gate. They had to walk in, so it might take several more days before they get back into town, especially if they got invited into the hunt club."

"I know you are right. I'm just on edge. I really want to see what they have done up there, and I kind of want to be a part of it, you know, rub elbows with some of their rich friends."

"Well, you are just going to have to wait or go talk with Mr. Amjad while he is still in Mirror Lake. After all, you were not aware that he was going to be at the grand opening for the gallery, so you could use that as an opening. And maybe he will invite you up without all this hoopla."

Henry says, "Well, maybe you are right about that. I can at least pay him a visit and mention seeing him at the gallery opening, and then maybe he will give me more info and invite me up."

CHAPTER 23

Denton makes his way over to the gallery after having breakfast at Maddie's Café. He figures Helen is probably there by now, and he wants to talk with her about the two gentlemen that were with Margaret at the opening on Saturday night. When Denton gets to the gallery, the doors are locked, but Helen walks up before he can turn to leave. Helen says, "Good morning, sheriff."

Denton grins. "So now it's sheriff not Denton?"

Helen just laughs. "Well, you are the sheriff, aren't you?"

"Well, yes, ma'am, I guess I'm."

They both laugh as Helen unlocks the door, and they walk in. Helen goes back toward the back of the gallery, and as she is putting her purse away, she turns to Denton and says, "What do I owe the pleasure of seeing you this early on Monday morning?"

Denton says, "Do I have to have a reason to see you on a Monday morning?"

Helen smiles. "No, I guess you don't. But if I had to guess, there is something on your mind." She can't help but think about their kiss on Saturday night, and she holds her breath.

Denton says, "I wanted to see your pretty face, and also I'm sorry to admit I wanted to ask you a few questions about the two gentlemen that were with Margaret at the gallery Saturday night."

Helen says, "So as I thought," with a grin. "I'm nothing more than a passing fancy."

"Darling, you are certainly more than a passing fancy, but we will get into that a little later. But I really do have some questions for you."

Helen realizes he is serious and wonders why so interested in Mr. Sommeren and Mr. Amjad. She says, "What kind of questions and why?"

Denton says, "I just wanted to know who they are and why they were there."

Helen says, "The taller gentlemen's name is Mr. J. Sommeren, and the other shorter fellow is a Mr. Ameer Amjad. They're the investors I told you about that are clients of Margaret's."

"Do you know where they're from? I understand the Middle East, but exactly where in the Middle East?"

Helen replies, "I think from Turkey but couldn't swear by that, why?"

Denton responds, "Well, Henry and Gordon seem to know them and were surprised to see them at the open house for the gallery. Henry mentioned something about Mr. Amjad leasing some property from him, way up in the northeast mountains of North Carolina. I just can't help but wonder why two men from the Middle East would want to lease land that far out into the wilderness. So I thought I would do a little checking up on them."

Helen says, "I can give Margaret a call and see what other information I can get on them if you would like?"

"Yes, I would like that if you don't mind. I just don't always trust Henry Mason, so I can't help but wonder what he might be up to."

Helen says, "I'll get back to you once I've talked with Margaret?"

Denton responds, "Thanks. Now with that out of the way, Mrs. Coleman, I just have to say again how great things were Saturday night with the opening and how beautiful you were, and I hope I didn't scare you off. How about lunch today at our favorite spot, Maddie's Café?"

Helen just looks into his eyes and says, "Thank you, and no, you didn't scare me off. And yes to lunch, what time would you like to meet?"

"Good, what about twelve-thirty?"

Helen replies, "That sounds good to me. See you then."

Denton leans down and gives her a little kiss on the check then turns and walks out the door. Helen just stands there for a few minutes, blushing.

After Helen gets settled in her office before she starts her Monday routine, she gives Margaret a call. Margaret answers the phone, "Good morning, sis, is everything okay up there?"

Helen says, "Yes, it is. I just have a few questions I would like to ask you regarding Mr. Sommeren and Mr. Amjad."

Margaret says, "Sure. What kind of questions?"

"Well, just wanted to know where they're from and then really anything that you know about them and their business in the US other than my gallery?"

"Okay, I know they're from Istanbul, Turkey. As far as their business, I just know that they contacted my firm, looking for help with investments in the area. Why all these questions now?"

Helen says, "Denton dropped by this morning and wanted to know what I knew about them. He says that Henry Mason and Gordon Grover were talking about them as though they knew them at the gallery open house on Saturday, and they seemed surprised that they were there. So he wants to do some background checking on them. But he didn't want to talk with Henry or Gordon about it at this time. When Denton asks Henry how he knew them on Saturday, Henry mentioned that Mr. Amjad leased some property of Henry's up in the northeast mountains out in the middle of nowhere. Denton just thinks that's odd for two men from the Middle East."

Margaret replies, "Well, you never know, and of course, Henry Mason isn't the most forthcoming person in Mirror Lake. Denton might do just as well to ask Henry what Mr. Amjad leased the land for."

"I agree. You've given me enough for now, and I'll let you know anything I find out on my in. Talk with you later, love you."

Margaret responds, "Love you too."

CHAPTER 24

Helen meets Denton for lunch at Maddie's, and while they're eating, she tells him that Margaret didn't have much information on the two men short of they're from Istanbul, Turkey. Pretty much all she has is that they contacted her firm, looking for help with investments in the area. She was not aware of any land leases they might have. Helen asks Denton, "What has peaked your interest in these two gentlemen?"

Denton says, "I'm not totally sure. It was just the way Henry and Gordon were talking then stopped talking, you know, they just looked funny. I just get a strange feeling sometimes, and when I do, I've to go with my instincts."

Helen isn't sure what to say about this, but she thinks it might have something to do with the attacks on 9/11. Helen says, "Then that's what you should do, do your background checking, then talk with Henry about this property that Mr. Amjad has leased."

Denton thanks Helen for checking with Margaret, and they finish their lunch. As they're leaving, Denton looks at Helen and says, "When can I see you again?"

Helen says, "When do you want to see me again?"

Denton laughs. "Okay, we sound like teenagers now. I want to see you tonight. Is that okay?"

Helen says, "Well, I'll have to check my calendar, but I believe I'm free. You want to drop by the gallery around six-thirty tonight, and I can let you know?"

Denton grins. "Okay, you want to play cat and mouse? I'm game if you are."

They both head their separate ways.

*****

Henry calls over to the resort to see if Mr. Amjad is still registered there and finds out that he is. Henry then asks to be connected to his room. Mr. Sommeren answers the phone, and Henry greets him with "Good morning, this is Henry Mason calling for Mr. Amjad. Is he in?"

Mr. Sommeren replies, "Yes, he is but not available to come to the phone at this time. May I take a message?"

Henry says, "Yes, just ask him if he is going to be in Mirror Lake awhile? I would like to meet with him. He can give me a call, and I can come to him, or he can drop by my office. He has my number."

Mr. Sommeren says, "I'll give him the message, and he will be in touch."

Henry says thanks and hangs up. Henry does not know what to think; he doesn't know anything about this Mr. Sommeren, but he assumes that he is Mr. Amjad's assistant or something. He will just have to wait and see what comes of all this, but he hopes that he will hear from Mr. Amjad before he leaves Mirror Lake.

Mr. Sommeren informs Mr. Amjad of the call from Henry, and Mr. Amjad asks what he wanted. Mr. Sommeren tells him he didn't say just that he would like to talk with him before he leaves Mirror Lake. Mr. Sommeren asks, "Did you mention anything to him about our dealings with Mrs. Coleman and the gallery?"

Mr. Amjad replies, "No, I saw no reason to. They're two different interests."

Mr. Sommeren says, "You don't always understand the ways of the Americans. This is a small community, and everyone knows everyone, so I'm certain he was surprised to see you at the opening of the gallery."

Mr. Amjad says, "I didn't think about that and what it might look like, but I'm not worried because the man, Henry Mason, is all about the money, and as long as nothing interferes with him getting what he wants, he will not care."

"I know you think you understand this man, but we need to be cautious about how we do business so no one becomes suspicious. So I believe it's wise to talk with this Henry Mason and let him know that you heard about the gallery through your financial advisor and decided that it would be a good investment and a way to introduce your arts and culture."

Mr. Amjad agrees and says he would call him.

*****

Gordon calls Henry to see if he had talked with Mr. Amjad, and if so, what did he get out of the conversation. Henry explains he didn't talk with him, just left a message asking that he meet with him before he left town. Henry asks Gordon if he had heard from the boys, and Gordon tells him not yet.

CHAPTER 25

Denton gets to the gallery about six-thirty, and Helen is still working with the receipts and other paperwork from the grand opening. Denton says, "Are you ready for dinner?"

Helen replies, "Yes, I still have work to do, but it can wait until tomorrow. Where are we going?"

Denton says, "I thought we might pick up some food and take out to my place and have a picnic on the lake."

Helen smiles. "That sounds nice. It stays light late enough now to enjoy the evening."

They leave and go by a little sandwich shop, which also carries wine and picks up what they want, then head out to Denton's. They walk down to the lake where Denton already has a picnic table set up. Helen looks over at him and says, "You had this already planned out, didn't you?"

Denton, with a wide grin, says, "Well, sort of, I really hoped you would say yes soon to another evening out."

Helen smiles. "I'm beginning to think you know me to well."

Denton says. "Not as well as I would like to know you."

Helen blushes, and they start putting out the food, and Helen works on changing the subject. But before she could, Denton says, "I'm sorry if I made you uncomfortable. That was not my intentions. I just really enjoy your company, and I'm not always good with words."

Helen replies, "You didn't. It's just it has been a long time since I've had this kind of a relationship. I, too, am not good with my words, and I enjoy your company as well. You are so easy to talk with. I feel like I've known you forever."

Denton says, "I feel the same, and I haven't had these kinds of feelings in a long time either. I didn't think I would ever have these kinds of feelings again. You just seem to make it so easy for me. I just don't know exactly where we go next. I know where I would like for it to go, but I don't want to scare you away or rush anything."

Helen responds, "I feel the same way, but I'm glad you don't want to rush things. I know we both have been through a lot, and I feel like we both want the same things. But at the same time, I believe it's better to get to know each other slowly. That way, no one gets hurt. Also I believe in always being straight forward and honest with my feelings, and I hope you'll be the same way."

Denton says, "I think that's what I really like about you, and why it's easy to be with you. I'm not a complicated man, and you make it easy for me to stay that way. Let's eat and enjoy the sunset."

Helen smiles and says, "Yes, that sounds great."

They finish their meal, and Denton builds a little fire while they sat on a blanket by the lake in each other's arms and enjoy the sunset. Later, Denton takes Helen back to town to her car and kisses her good night, and they both head home.

When Helen gets home, she calls Margaret to tell her about her evening with Denton. Margaret asks, "So how do you really feel about this man?"

Helen says, "I really like him. He is everything I could ever want. I'm just not sure if it's right for me to want a relationship at my age."

Margaret says, "Okay, you are not dead. You're not even that old. Having a relationship with him does not mean you have to marry him. He hasn't mentioned marriage, has he?"

Helen laughs. "No, he hasn't, and I know I can like him and even have a relationship with out marrying him. It's just a little scary, that's all."

Margaret says, "It's just because it has been a long time since you had a relationship with anyone other than Gus, so I understand it being scary. I just say go with it and see where it leads."

Helen laughs. "I know you are right, and that's why I called you and why I love you. Good night, and I'll talk with you in a few days."

Margaret replies, "Good night and sweet dreams," then laughs.

CHAPTER 26

Mr. Amjad gives Henry Mason a call and sets up a lunch meeting with him on Wednesday, twenty-second, at the resort restaurant. He and Mr. Sommeren have talked it over, and Mr. Amjad realizes that it's important for him to explain why he was at the gallery grand opening, and that it doesn't have anything to do with his business with Henry—that he is just interested in art and sharing their cultures.

Henry gives Gordon a call on Tuesday to let him know about his meeting with Mr. Amjad on Wednesday and asks if he would like to be at said meeting. Gordon tells him he would and gets the time and place. Henry asks Gordon, "Have you heard anything from the boys?"

Gordon replies, "No, I haven't, and I'm getting a little worried, but let's wait until after our meeting with Mr. Amjad on Wednesday before we really start to panic, okay?"

Henry says, "Okay, I agree. That will be a week by then, and if they haven't returned by Wednesday, or we haven't heard from them, we will have to make a decision on what to do. I'm not sure how we could check on them if they're not answering their cells."

Gordon says, "I know. I've thought about that as well. I guess we could go to the sheriff and see what he thinks."

"Well, I really hate to involve him in this, but we might not have a choice. But I tell you this, if we do that and then we find out that these two idiots are just out drinking and partying, I'll kill them myself."

Gordon says, "I know they're a little immature, but I don't think they would do that."

"I hope not. I don't want anything to mess up our business with Mr. Amjad. And I don't want it all over town that we have leased this land to Mr. Amjad. He's made it clear that he likes his privacy, so I want to make sure that happens. I don't want a lot of people pestering him or trying to go to the hunt club without an invite from Mr. Amjad. You haven't mentioned it to anyone, have you?"

Gordon says, "Of course not. I don't care about the hunt club short of the money we are getting, or should I say recouping on our own investment in that hunt club."

Henry thinks he is glad to hear Gordon say that as long as he does not think a lot about it and is happy with the money then all should be well.

Mr. Sommeren and Mr. Amjad talk about their plans; they plan on leaving Wednesday afternoon. Going up to the camp, they want to see who all is there. There are a number of their people that were flying into Atlanta from various places in the Middle East and then renting vehicles and heading straight to the camp. If everyone has arrived, then they can have discussions regarding their plans for the target and timing and if they want to think about moving the date up from September 11 to an earlier date. Mr. Sommeren still believes that if they're as far ahead of schedule as they appear to be at this time, it's very important that they move the date up. He is afraid if they don't, it will leave them open to discovery, especially since they have already had one incident with the two Americans that wondered near and have been killed. He is afraid the longer they wait with these two men missing that someone may come looking for them, and he isn't sure they can convince anyone that the camp is truly a hunt club.

*****

Denton is setting in his office, thinking about these two men, Mr. Sommeren and Mr. Amjad, and is wondering who he still knows in New York either with the NYPD or Homeland Security. He knows if there is still someone in one of these offices, he knows he has a means of getting a better background check on them. The first name that comes to mind is Jack Abrams; he used to be commissioner of the NYPD before he moved over to Homeland Security. He will have to give Jack a call. To do this, he will have to go through his old files and information that he brought with him from New York after he gets home. But before going home, he thinks he will pick up a couple of coffees and drop in on Helen at the gallery.

CHAPTER 27

It's Wednesday the twenty-second, and Mr. Amjad is setting in the restaurant at the resort, waiting for Henry when Henry and Gordon walk up to the table. Henry says, "Good afternoon, Mr. Amjad, you remember Gordon Grover?"

Mr. Amjad replies, "Yes, nice to see you both. Please sit, we can order before we begin."

Henry and Gordon sit as a waitress walks up to take their order. Once she's walked away, Henry jumps right in saying, "It was nice to see you Saturday night at our little gallery opening. I hope you enjoyed it."

Mr. Amjad replies, "Yes, I did. I always enjoy culture and the arts."

"I wasn't aware that you knew about our little gallery much less about its grand opening. I was not expecting you to be back in Mirror Lake this soon. I figured you were either back home or possibly at the hunt club."

"I learned about the gallery through my financial group, Gilpin, Grays and Connor in Atlanta. Once I heard it was in Mirror Lake, I couldn't resist. It gave me an opportunity for another investment just using some art and sculptures from my own country, which always makes me happy."

Henry looks at Gordon with a funny look on his face, but Gordon does not see the implications of what Mr. Amjad has just said. Henry says, "That sounds wonderful. We always like diversity in our little town. I must ask how is the hunt club coming along? Have you had the opportunity to go on a hunt yet, or are you still working on the improvements you were going to make on the property?"

Mr. Amjad realizes that Henry, in his roundabout way, is asking what he's done to the property. He answers, "We didn't do many changes at all, so we were able to do them ourselves without having to hire anyone. We haven't had our first hunt yet but hope to soon. I'm headed up to the hunt club this very afternoon. If you wish, I'll send you a memo with all of the changes we have made?"

"That will not be necessary. Maybe a little later I can join you on one of your hunts?"

Mr. Amjad is taken back on this comment but smiles and says, "Most certainly…once we are a little more established."

They finish their meal and say their goodbyes, and Henry and Gordon rise and leave the table. Once they're out of earshot, Henry looks at Gordon and says, "Did you hear what he said?"

Gordon says, "Well, I heard the conversation, but what part are you talking about?"

"The part about investing in the gallery and the name of the financial group in Atlanta. I believe that's the same financial group that Margaret O'Keefe works for. So that would be why they were with her Saturday night."

Gordon says, "So what is the problem?"

"Well, I'm not sure, but we really didn't want anyone to know about our leasing the property to Mr. Amjad."

"And again why does that matter?"

Henry says, "Because we don't want a lot of people disturbing him at the hunt club."

Gordon replies, "I think you worry too much about this. Mr. Amjad appears very capable of taking care of himself. I'm sure if he does not want someone at the hunt club, he knows how to deal with that."

Henry says, "Okay, I guess you are right. I do worry too much. I just don't want anything to upset the applecart."

Gordon says, "Well, you have a working contract with him, so if he decided to back out for whatever reason, you are covered, right?"

Henry laughs and says, "Yeah, you are right. We do have a contract. Okay, it's Wednesday, and you or I neither one has heard anything form Chuck and Donald, so what do you think we should do?"

Gordon says, "Well again, I tried both cell numbers this morning, and it's like they're dead or broken. So the only thing I can think of is to go to the sheriff."

Henry says, "I really don't want to do that at least not yet. I've been thinking we are not even sure they went up there. Maybe they just decided to take the money you gave them and go on a little vacation. So I say let's leave it alone for a little longer and see what happens. But if they show up and that's what they have done, they will owe the money back with interest."

Gordon says, "Okay, we will wait, and if they don't show soon, someone will come looking for them, but no one knows to come to us."

CHAPTER 28

Denton gets to the gallery just as Helen is locking up. Helen says, "Hi there, where are you headed?"

Denton grins and says, "To see you. I've a couple of coffees. Want to go somewhere and sit for a bit?"

Helen says, "Yes, that sounds nice."

They head over to the little park between Main Street and the resort and find a nice spot on a swing and sit with their coffees and talk. Denton asks, "How about coming out to my place Friday night and have dinner?"

Helen says, "Only if we can watch the sun set by the lake with a little fire like we did the last time."

Denton says, "I think I can make that happen with no problem. Is it okay if I cook up some pork chops on the grill with a few veggies as well?"

Helen says, "That sounds good. It's a date!"

Denton asks her, "Have you talked with Margaret lately? Any chance she's gotten any more information on this Mr. Sommeren and Mr. Amjad?"

Helen replies, "No, I haven't talked with her again, but I believe she would have called if anything had turned up. You really have a bad feeling about these men, don't you?"

Denton says, "Yeah, and I can't quite put my finger on it. Something just does not feel right."

Helen says, "Does it have to do with what you went through on 9/11?"

Denton gets very quiet and looks straight ahead for a few minutes.

Helen says, "I'm sorry I should not have brought up 9/11. I know that had to be a very hard time, and I don't mean to pry."

Denton looks at Helen and says, "No, that's okay. I've got to be able to talk about it at some point. You are right. It's hard, and I'm not sure that's why I've got this feeling about these men or not. But if I've learned anything in this life, it's to always listen to my gut, and my gut is telling me something is off with these two men. I've got a friend that used to work with the NYPD, and I believe is now with Homeland Security, so I plan to give him a call and see if he will run a background check on them. He has better access for the kind of background check I would need."

Helen says, "What kind of things are you looking for?"

Denton replies, "You look for business ties in different countries and money movement, also to see if their business is truly legitimate. Those are the kind of things you would look for that might signal terrorist links, and sometimes you come across other associates of theirs that are flagged for terrorist links as well."

Helen says, with tears stinging her eyes, "That all sounds so scary. I don't even like to think about it, but I have to say I'm glad that there are people like you that do think about it. It certainly makes me feel a little safer, and when or if you are ever ready to talk about 9/11, I'm a great listener."

Denton looks at her and says, "That's nice to know. I know there will come a time that I need to talk about it. But I also know it will not be easy, but I can say I know you'll help make it easy." Then Denton leans down and kisses her softly.

They finish their coffee and head their separate ways.

It's Sunday afternoon, and Helen is at home, enjoying her quiet time with a good book when her phone rings, and it's Margaret. Margaret says, "Hi, sis, what's going on with you today? I'm surprised to find you home and not out with Denton."

Helen laughs and says, "No, I was out at his place on Friday and had dinner and saw him just a few minutes yesterday, so today I'm enjoying doing nothing other than reading a good book and spending a little time with mom."

Margaret says, "Speaking of mom, how is she doing?"

Helen says, "She is doing good…just stays at home most of the time. She goes to church and to her women's club middle of the week, and that makes her happy."

"Now to the good part, how are things going with you and Denton. Have we gotten to the good parts yet?"

Helen laughs. "Well, it depends on what you consider the good parts. We've talked but have decided to take it slow. We both agree we are looking for the same thing."

Margaret jumps in and says, "And what might that be? Just for someone to talk to or something more?"

Helen says, "I think we both are looking for something more. Having said that, I think it's going to be easier for me than for Denton. I think Denton enjoys my company, and I believe he is interested in something more physical but still hurting emotional. So going slow will be good for him and safe for me."

"That sounds good, at least you are ready to move on, and I really think there is no one better than you to help him move on. I'll let you get back to your book and talked with you soon. Love you, sis."

Helen says, "Love you to. Later."

CHAPTER 29

Mr. Sommeren and Mr. Amjad leave Mirror Lake and headed toward the camp. Once they get there, they find that everyone has arrived. And actually no one came through Mirror Lake, which is good for them. That way no one in Mirror Lake, especially noisy Henry Mason, knows how many people are at what they call the hunt club. Everything seems to be organized and ready for their meeting, so they can finalize their plans for this attack on Washington DC. They have a number of scenarios they have put together, and now they have to decide which one will be the most effective with the most impact and then pick the right date which may need to be before 9/11/02.

It's now May 27, Memorial Day, and Mirror Lake is having their annual Memorial Day celebration on the lake. Everyone gets together and has a big picnic lunch with all kinds of food and games for the kids, and to end it all, there is a big fireworks show around nine to nine-thirty that night. This event has been a part of Mirror Lake for as long as Helen can remember. This will be Denton's first Mirror Lake Memorial Day, and Helen plans on making him feel right at home.

Meanwhile, up at the camp, Mr. Amjad and Mr. Sommeren is having their last meeting; today they will make their final decision. Mr. Sommeren says, "The plan we all seem to like is the best plan we could have. It's using two attacks simultaneously on the National Mall of Washington, bombs for the west end of the National Mall and chemicals on the east end of the National Mall closes to the Capitol. It will create utter chaos. They will not know which way to turn. On one end will be fire and brimstone, and on the other, people will just fall in their tracks. It will be an incredible day. The infidels will never forget, and if we move our attack date up to the fourth of July, it will be most effective."

Mr. Amjad says, "I still like the date of 9/11. It's more significant."

Mr. Sommeren says, "But it's more than two months away from the date of July 4, and they will be more people there on July 4 than on September 11. I believe the longer we wait, the greater chance we might be discovered. We have been so blessed to get this far and be ready that we must take advantage of this great opportunity now. We don't want to miss our chance at our good fortune."

Everyone is in agreement that using this tactic is the best and most effective way to go, and so Mr. Amjad finally comes around to changing the date to July 4. They're ready to celebrate their good fortune and praise Allah.

Back at Mirror Lake, they're wrapping up the festivities, and everyone is headed home. Denton looks at Helen and says, "I know it's late, but why don't you come home with me for a while?"

Helen looks up at him and isn't sure what to say or do. She isn't actually sure what he is asking.

Denton says, "Well, what do you say? I've just enjoyed this day so much I just don't want it to end…please."

Helen smiles and says, "Okay, but I'll drive my car so you don't have to come back into town."

They leave, and Helen follows him out to his place. Once they get there, they set on his porch in a swing, and for a little while are just quietly sitting there holding hands. Denton says, "This is so nice. It has been so long since I've felt this content, and it's all because of you."

"I feel the same, however, I believe that this place is also beginning to get to you. It has that effect on people. It's so calm and slow, not fast pace the entire time, so people stop to smell the roses so to speak. It's a kind of a euphoria of since."

Denton agrees but then says, "But it's mostly you. My wife was very much like you. She was always my calming effect after a storm. She could take a bad day and make the ending the most wonderful thing."

Helen is just quite; she isn't sure what to say. Denton blushes and says, "I'm sorry I didn't mean to upset you."

Helen says, "Oh, you didn't upset me. I'm glad you feel like you can say anything to me. You have to remember I, too, feel a loss. My husband and I didn't always get along. We had our good years and our bad years. We ended on a good year. He always had a way of making me feel safe just like you do. And I knew we could just be together and didn't always have to talk. Those are the things I like about you. These are the things that make me happy."

Denton takes her in his arms and kisses her long and hard, and she kisses him back. Then he whispers in her ear, "Stay the night with me," and they go inside, and the lights go out.

The next morning, Helen comes into the kitchen, and Denton has already made the coffee and is cooking eggs and bacon at the stove. He says, "Good morning, did you sleep well?"

Helen smiles and says, "Who slept?" then she laughs and says, "Yes, how about you?"

Denton grins. "When I slept, it was like a baby." He turns and takes her in his arms and kisses her softly and says, "Last night was wonderful, thank you. I hope I haven't gotten you into trouble with your mother."

Helen laughs. "You're okay. Number one, she loves you, and number 2, she sleeps like a rock, so if I get home in the next forty-five minutes, she will never know I was not there."

Denton says, "Well, let's have a bit of breakfast and get you out of here."

They finish up, and Denton just puts the dishes in the sink, and they both head out.

CHAPTER 30

Denton gets into his office and sees he's a message from Jack Abrams. He had called last Friday and left a message, asking Jack to run a background check on Mr. Sommeren and Mr. Amjad. The message from Jack was asking Denton to please call him back. Denton picks up the phone and gives Jack a call. "Good morning, Jack, hope you had a good holiday weekend."

Jack replies, "I did, how about you?"

Denton replies, "It couldn't have been any better."

Jack asks, "So does that mean that small town life and being out in the country agrees with you? You don't miss the big city life and the pace in the fast lane?"

Denton replies, "Not at all, and the scenery up here is pretty terrific as well. So you got my message about the background check, and have you found out anything?"

Jack asks, "What is giving you the cause to need a background check on these two men?"

"Not really sure, just a gut feeling."

Jack says, "That's good enough for me. I've run a background check with every agency data network I could find using only their names and city and country they're from. Nothing much is showing up other than they appear to have money and dabble in the arts. Haven't found much else, but it will require more information from you such as fingerprints or even better DNA, then I could run them through AFIS and CODIS. I've also run their names through Interpol, nothing there, at least not yet to go on. Do you happen to have photos of them?"

"Sorry, no, I don't but may be able to get my hands on at least photos. I'll do a little more checking and get back to you."

Jack says, "Sounds good. I know you would not be asking these questions if you were not concerned. But try not to let your emotions play into your feelings toward these two men just because they're Middle Eastern."

"I know, and I really don't believe it has. I can't tell you actually what it is yet, give me a little more time, and we will see if it's really anything or just me. Thanks, Jack, I knew you would do this for me and not judge me. You're a good friend. Talk with you soon."

"Will be waiting to hear back from you. Take care, my friend."

Denton decides to go pick up a couple of coffees and head over to the gallery to see Helen. She should be in by now, he thinks. He wants to see if they had anyone taking pictures at the galleries grand opening, and if they did, just maybe he will have some good photos of this Mr. Sommeren and Mr. Amjad. Denton gets to the gallery and walks in and back to Helen's office; she is busy going over their list of inventory, getting ready to set more things out when she looks up, and Denton is standing in the doorway, smiling. Helen says, "Just can't stay away from me, can you?"

Denton smiles back and says, "No, I can't. Need more coffee?"

Helen says, "How did you know? Was it the lack of sleep last night?" then she blushes.

Denton says, "Well, if you are as tired as I am, then that would be a good indication that you need more coffee." Denton hands her coffee and sits in a chair in front of her desk. He looks at her and says, "I also have a few question for you about the galleries grand opening night."

"Sure, what's on your mind?"

"Well, you know I had a background check run on Mr. Sommeren and Mr. Amjad, right now nothing much is coming up."

Helen breaks in and says, "Well, that's good, isn't it?"

"Yes, to a degree. However, all I had to go on was their names and city and country they're from. That's not enough to do what we would consider a full background check. It would be great if we had fingerprints or DNA, but the next best thing would be photos. I was thinking that we just might have that if you had someone taking pictures at the galleries opening."

"Well, yes, we did. I haven't gotten them back yet, but will check and see if they're ready, and if they are, I'll pick them up and come over to your office, and we can go through them together."

"That sounds great. I guess I need to let you get back to work, and I need to get on with my day. See you later?"

"Most certainly, but it will be after lunch."

Before Helen could make her call to Photos by Art, who took the pictures for the grand opening, her phone rings. Helen answers, "Mirror Lake's Arts and Antiquities, Helen speaking."

Margaret says, "Well, hello, Ms. Helen with Mirror Lake's Arts and Antiquities, how are you today?"

Helen laughs and says, "Well, I'm fine, and how is my little sister this fine Tuesday morning?"

Margaret is smiling to herself and thinking the weekend must have gone well and then says, "I'm fine, but you sound tired but great. So tell me all about your weekend."

Helen says, "I swear you have some kind of sixth sense about you. You seem to know just when to ask your questions," and then Helen laughs.

"Well, spill the beans, I want all the details even the nasty ones, leave nothing out."

Helen can't help but smile. "It was wonderful. Denton and I spent the day together on Memorial Day through all of the festivities, including the fireworks. Then he asks me to go home with him for a while, and I did."

Margaret says, "Okay, that's not all I can tell by the sound of your voice, so you better continue. I want it all."

"We sit on his front porch in his swing, just holding hands for a while, and he started talking about how I'm like his wife but in a good way. I let him know I understood and felt the same. That he makes me feel safe and happy. Then we kiss and go inside, and I stayed the night with him. Do you think that was wrong of me?"

She has a little crack in her voice. Margaret says, "Of course not, sis, it makes you a woman again. That's all. Do you really like him? And is he good to you?"

"Yes, I do really like him, and I don't think he could be any better to me. I just feel like I'm letting everyone down because Gus hasn't been gone all that long."

Margaret replies, "Gus has been gone over a year, and you don't owe anyone anything but yourself. So I say go for it if he makes you happy. You don't even have to get married unless that's what both of you want."

"I do believe that's what both of us will want in time, but it's nice to have someone to talk with and sometimes just to be with and not have to talk. We seem to love the same things."

"Then I think you have finally awakened, my big sister."

They both say their goodbyes and hang up.

CHAPTER 31

Helen calls Photos by Art to see if her pictures of the gallery opening are ready. They tell her yes, and she says she will come by after lunch to pick them up. Helen works in the gallery for several more hours, then around 1:00 p.m., leaves to go pick up her pictures. Once Helen has the pictures, she stops by Maddie's Café and picks up a couple of plates for her and Denton, then heads over to his office. Helen walks in, and Denton gets up. "What do you have here?" and goes over to take the food out of her hands.

Helen says, "Thanks. That was a little heavier than I thought it would be. Hope you haven't had lunch yet."

"No, I haven't, and I'm really hungry. Thanks for this, I owe you."

"Don't worry. Happy to do it, and believe me, I'll collect."

Denton laughs, then they sit at his desk and eat before looking over the pictures she's brought.

Once they had finished their meal, Helen takes the pictures out of here purse and hands them over to Denton. He splits half with her, and they start looking through them. Every once in a while, they show a photo to each other and talk about it or who it's of. Finally, Denton comes across one of Helen, Margaret, Mr. Sommeren, and Mr. Amjad, and he thinks this one might work. They keep looking, but it seems like all of the others were not straight on shots, so it would not work for facial recognition. Denton tells Helen he will keep the one of the four of them to see if it will work. Helen tells him that's fine and hopes it will do what he needs it to.

Helen says, "I need to get back to work. Talk with you later. Let me know what comes of this, okay?"

Denton says, "Of course, I will. I'll call you tonight."

After Helen has gone, Denton picks up the phone and calls Jack Abrams. Jack picks up and says, "Hi, buddy, didn't expect to hear back from you this quick. Got something for me?"

Denton replies, "Yeah, I've a photo of the two men, but it has two other people in it. Will that work?"

Jack says, "Yes, depending if it's a clear picture and straight on for the facial recognition to work. What I'll do is cut the two men out of the picture and run them one at a time. So fax the picture over to me, and I'll get back to you as soon as I've got something."

Denton says, "Will do and look forward to hearing from you. Again, thanks, Jack, I really appreciate this." Denton then faxes over the picture and hopes it will either tell him something good or something bad, so he can let this go.

Denton gets a call from Sheriff Thornton in a neighboring town called Deer Creek. He is calling about two young men from his town that has been reported missing. Their names are Chuck Anderson and Donald Dawson. Denton tells him he's heard nothing about the two men, but that if he will fax over some info, he will put some flyers out around Mirror Lake and do some checking with the people in Mirror Lake. Sheriff Thornton faxes over the information, and Denton has one of his men type up the flyer, then they post them around town and ask if anyone has seen or heard anything of these two missing men to contact the sheriff's office.

Denton goes over to the G&G Bar and Gill and asks Gordon if it's okay to put up one of the flyers. Gordon looks at the flyer and almost swallows his tongue. It takes him a minute to answer Denton, so Denton says, "Are you okay, Gordon? You look like you have seen a ghost."

Gordon swallows hard and says, "Oh uh, I'm okay, and sure, you can put it up right over there. That way, it will be seen by everyone that comes in."

Denton says, "Thanks. Are you sure you are okay? Do you know these two young men?"

Gordon still looks kind of funny but says, "No, I don't think I do. It's just a bad thing if someone goes missing."

Denton says, "Thanks again," and leaves.

Gordon couldn't wait for him to get out of the door quick enough before he looks at his bartender and says, "I've got to run an errand. Be back in a bit." Gordon goes just about as fast as he can straight to Henry's office and goes right in without stopping at his secretary's desk.

Henry is surprised and looks at Gordon and says, "What the hell is wrong with you?"

Gordon can't talk; he is breathing so hard. He sits down and catches his breath before trying speaking. Finally Gordon says, "Chuck and Donald have been reported missing. The sheriff just put up a flyer in my bar about them. What are we going to do?"

Henry, looking strange, says, "Nothing at the moment."

Gordon says, "But we have to. What if something bad has happened to them."

Henry says, "What could possibly bad have happened to them? The people at the hunt club are not bad people. So they're missing. It has only been about two weeks, and we don't even know if they went up to the hunt club. My guess is that they didn't and instead took the money you gave them and like I said before went on a little vacation."

Gordon says, "I didn't give them that much money. It was only $100. I told them they would get more once they came back. So I don't think they would have just gone off and not come back to collect the rest of the money. Now do you...they may not be very bright, but $100 isn't much."

Henry says, "Okay, just calm down. I need to think. I mean we don't know much other than they were going up into the northeast corner of the mountains. I just don't want to make a big thing out of this and upset Mr. Amjad and have all this county law enforcement running all over the place up there."

Gordon says, "Well, I don't want to be a party to something bad. So I say we give it the rest of the day, and if nothing else has come of all this, then we talk to Sheriff Gage."

"Okay, in the morning, if no one has heard from them, you and I'll talk again and decided what to do."

CHAPTER 32

Denton goes back to his office and can't get the way Gordon responded to the flyer out of his mind. He thinks back on the conversation he overheard between Henry and Gordon at the gallery grand opening. It just makes this feeling he has even worst. There is something up with Henry, Gordon, and this Mr. Sommeren and Mr. Amjad; he just can't imagine what it could be. Thinking of Henry Mason, it has to have something to do with money. But what other than the money he and Gordon are making off of the lease of his property could it be? He keeps going back to why two Middle Eastern men would want to be in the North Carolina mountains in the wilderness. He just does not see it.

Helen finishes up at the shop and heads home. She keeps thinking about Denton and his concern over Mr. Sommeren and Mr. Amjad. She decides to give Margaret a call once she gets home and see if by chance she's found out anything else. Once Helen is at home and has had dinner with her mother, she goes back to her room and gives Margaret a call. Margaret answers, "Hello there, sis, I thought you would be busy instead of calling me this early."

"No, I came home after work and had dinner with mom, and she, of course, has already turned in for the night. I'm calling to see if you found out anything more about Mr. Sommeren and or Mr. Amjad?"

Margaret replies, "No, I ask one of our partners if we had any other information on these gentlemen that I don't already have, and he said no but was curious as to why I wanted to know."

Helen asks, "What did you tell him?"

Margaret says, "That since they were investing in Mirror Lake Arts and Antiquities, which is owned by my sister, that I was just curious."

"And he bought that?"

"Yes, and actually there isn't anything more I could tell him, is there? I mean Denton doesn't know anything more, does he?"

Helen says, "No, but he really is trying to find out more. He got a picture from me today that was taken at the gallery opening of you, me, Mr. Sommeren, and Mr. Amjad."

Margaret breaks in and says, "What? What is he going to do with that?"

Helen replies, "Well, he's already had a friend at Homeland Security do a background check on them just using their names, city, and country, and that didn't amount to anything, so he's sent this photo to the same fellow, and he is going to run it through facial recognition to see if that brings up anything."

Margaret says, "Is he really that concerned with these two men? I mean I know they're from the Middle East, but obviously they're not on any watch list, or they would have never gotten into the country much less be able to invest in anything, don't you think?"

"Yes, I agree, but I also know that something is really bothering Denton, and he needs to scratch this itch he has."

"I don't mean to be insensitive, but does this have anything to do with his experience with 9/11?"

Helen replies, "No, I really don't think it does, but I know Denton, and if there isn't anything there, then he will let it go, and no harm, no foul. So don't worry, little sister, it will not come back on you or your work, okay?"

"Oh, honey, I'm not worried about that. However, I do worry about you, and don't get me wrong, I really like Denton, but I hope this isn't a problem because if it is, he will never be able to move on."

"I know and truly don't believe it is, not saying that they're being from the Middle East does not trigger something, but I do really believe he can move on."

Margaret says, "I know you, and I believe if anyone can help him do that, it's you, and I do believe that's what he's looking for. I really love you, sis, so you take care and call me anytime day or night."

"Love you too and thanks for always being there."

At this, they hang up, and Helen gets ready for bed; she is lying there reading when her phone rings, and it's Denton. Helen answers, "Hi there, are you home or still at the office?"

Denton says, "I'm home, just sitting on the porch in our favorite spot, thinking about you."

"Really? What were you thinking?"

"How I wish you were here with me and in my arms. You know you could come on out. I promise you would be home in the morning before your mother gets up."

Helen laughs. "I'm sure I could be, but sorry, I'm already in my pj's and in bed."

"Well, I could be there in twenty minutes, and I promise I would be out before your mother gets up."

Helen says, "You are a really bad boy, and I'm sure you would be out before mother got up, but not tonight. How about dinner at your place tomorrow night, and I'll bring the food. You can provide the entertainment."

Denton laughs and says, "That's a date, and now I'll say good night and go in and take a cold shower."

Helen laughs and hangs up.

CHAPTER 33

Wednesday, May 29, comes and goes, and there has been no word from Chuck or Donald. It's now Friday, May 31, and Gordon is getting really antsy because Henry has been avoiding him, not answering calls or not in his office. Gordon is thinking about going to talk to the sheriff anyway. He knows Henry will really be pissed, but he can't get Chuck and Donald out of his mind and will really feel bad if something happens or has happened to them. So Gordon decides that today is the day that he is going to talk to Denton no matter what Henry thinks, but he decides to go by Henry's office one last time to give him the opportunity to go with him. He gets to Henry's office, and his secretary tells him that Henry has gone out of town. Gordon asks when he left and where he went. She tells him that he left early this morning, and she was not sure where he was going, just that he would be back on Monday, June 3. Gordon is really mad that Henry didn't call him before going out of town, so he heads straight over to Denton's office.

Denton is setting at his desk, doing some paperwork when Gordon walks in, and Denton looks up and says, "Good morning, Gordon, what can I do for you today?"

Gordon just stands there for a few minutes and says nothing.

Denton says, "Is there something on your mind that I can help you with?"

Gordon clears his throat and sits down in a chair in front of Denton's desk and says, "Yeah, I need to tell you something. I lied when I told you I didn't know those two young men that are reported missing."

Denton says, "Really, do tell. I'm listening."

"Well, me and Henry hired them to go up to the northeast corner of the mountains where Henry owns a piece of property that was once a hunt club."

Denton breaks in and says, "This is the property that Henry has leased to this Mr. Amjad correct?"

Gordon replies, "Yes, it is. We ask these two boys to go up there and just look around because these fellows are supposed to have set it back up for hunting. They were going to do some work on the place and then have their own controlled hunts with some of their rich buddies from all over the world. But we haven't heard anything from Chuck or Donald since they left, which was on May 15 or there about."

Denton says, "Do they have cell phones?"

"Yes, but the coverage up there is spotty at best, and I haven't been able to reach them at all."

"Where is Henry? Why is he not here with you?"

"He left town this morning, and I don't know where he went. His secretary said she didn't know where he went just that he would be back on Monday."

Denton runs his hands through his hair in frustration and says, "You should have said something the other day when I was in your bar. Who knows what kind of trouble these boys are in?"

Gordon looks down and says, "I know. I'm sorry, but Henry didn't want to upset this Mr. Amjad because he really likes his privacy."

Denton couldn't help but think and wonder why that is. Then he thinks about Jack Abrams, and that he hasn't heard back from him regarding the facial recognition on these two men. Denton picks up his phone and calls Jack.

Jack answers, "You must be a mind reader. I was just about to call you."

Denton says, "Really? Does it have anything to do with that photo?"

"Yeah, it sure does. We got a hit on this Mr. Amjad, and it has turned out to be a dozy."

"Okay, give it to me because I've another development here that I believe is linked to them."

"Really? Well, listen, I'll be there tomorrow around noon, and I'm not coming alone. We may have stumbled on to something big."

Denton can't believe his ears; he doesn't know what to ask next. But before he can say anything, Jack says, "Don't worry. We will put all of this together when I get there tomorrow."

"Okay, see you then. Let me know if you need anything before getting here."

"Fine. See you soon."

Denton looks at Gordon and says, "You did the right thing by coming to me. Now I just wished you had done it sooner."

Gordon says, "I'm truly sorry, but I'll do anything you want and help in anyway. Just let me know."

"Go back to work, but don't say anything about this to anyone, let alone Henry."

Gordon says, "I promise I won't. Thanks, Denton."

Denton nods, and Gordon walks out the door.

Denton's day is done, and he heads out the door with so much on his mind he's almost forgotten that Helen is coming over for dinner. He hopes she will stay the night; he really needs to talk to someone he knows he can trust.

Helen has left the gallery early and gone home for just a bit before heading out to Denton's. She wanted to change into jeans and pack an overnight bag. While heading through town, she stops and picks up Chinese food and goes on to Denton's. When she gets there, he is sitting on the porch swing, lost in thought. He didn't even realize she had gotten there when she spoke, and it startled him. Helen says, "You okay? You look a little out of sorts?"

Denton says, "Yeah," and rises and pulls her into his arms and kisses her then says, "Glad you are here."

She holds up the bag with food in it and says, "Okay, then let's eat and then talk about what is bothering you."

They go inside and sit at his kitchen table and start eating. Once they're through, they sit in his den together on the sofa, and Helen says, "Okay, start talking and don't tell me there isn't anything wrong. I think I know you well enough now to know when something is bothering you."

Denton starts telling her about the missing boys, and of course, she's already seen the flyers, but he continues. He tells her about Gordon coming to see him today and about how Gordon and Henry hired the boys to go up into the northeast corner of the North Carolina mountains to look around the property that this Mr. Sommeren and Mr. Amjad leased from Henry and how Gordon and Henry haven't heard a word from them. Also that Henry left town this morning, and no one knows where he went. Then he tells her about his conversation with Jack Abrams, and that he will be in Mirror Lake by noon tomorrow.

Helen's mouth is open when Denton finally stops talking, and she says, "Oh my god, what does all of this mean?"

"Jack isn't sure, but I knew my gut wasn't wrong."

They talk more, and then Denton asks, "Can you stay the night?"

"I came prepared. My bag is in the car."

Denton goes out to get the bag, and they turn in. Neither of them feel amorous tonight; they both just need to be held.

CHAPTER 34

When Henry got up on Friday morning, May 31, he decides he is going to call Mr. Amjad and go up to the hunt club just to look around and see what they have done. He feels that since he owns the property that's his right. Also maybe he can find out if they have seen Chuck or Donald, but, of course, he will not ask, just wants to see if they mention the boys. He also decides not to tell Gordon about it until he is back in Mirror Lake. Matter fact, he isn't telling anyone about where he is going, of course, there is no one else to tell other than Gordon. He tries to call Mr. Amjad but gets no answer, then he remembers the cell service up there isn't good. He doesn't take anything with him, just climbs in his jeep and leaves around 8:30 a.m. He figures he will be back before Gordon starts calling him again.

When Henry gets within several miles of the hunt club, the spotters that are around the property radios in to let them know that someone is approaching. Once they describe him and the jeep, Mr. Sommeren realizes that it's Henry Mason. Even though they have tried to disguise the camp as a hunt club, he is afraid they have fallen short, and that Henry will get suspicious, and that will cause yet another problem. This is actually what he was afraid of. The two young boys were one thing, but Henry Mason, the mayor of Mirror Lake, would be another. It would be certain he would be missed. He goes to talk with Mr. Amjad quickly before Henry gets there.

Mr. Amjad says, "Have them bring him straight to me from the gate. Tell them not to deviate no matter what. Hopefully I can talk with him and satisfy whatever he is trying to find out. If I can, then he will leave, no more the wiser." Mr. Sommeren isn't sure about this but is sure they can't afford to kill or keep him there that long without someone missing him.

Henry gets to the hunt club and finds the gate locked—of course, with different locks than the ones he had on it and also that there are guards. They open the gate, and Mr. Sommeren is there to escort him straight to Mr. Amjad. Henry thinks this is kind of strange but realizes they're from a different culture and also that Mr. Amjad really likes his privacy. Henry is thinking that he will explain that he tried to call but couldn't get through. He is looking around and does not see any real changes other than to the gate and fence around the compound. He can't help but think why so much security for a hunt club. But as soon as he is greeted by Mr. Amjad, he forgets all of that.

Mr. Amjad says, "Hello, Mr. Mason, I was not expecting you. Is there something wrong?"

Henry replies, "No, not at all. I just thought I would come up and see how things were going. I first tried to call, however, couldn't get an answer and then remembered that the cell service isn't good up here. I thought that since I drove all the way up here, I would take a look around and see what changes you have made."

Mr. Amjad says, "Well, we really didn't make any to the buildings, just did better security."

"Yes, I noticed a lot of security for just a hunt club, don't you think?"

Mr. Amjad replies, "Well, we have guests that take their security very seriously. They come from all parts of the world that this kind of thing is very necessary. So we have obliged them this."

Henry says, "So you have had or are about to have your first hunt?"

Mr. Amjad replies, "Yes, we have had one. Unfortunately not very successful but are planning another within a few days. I would invite you to join. However, these particular guests are very private and would not appreciate an outsider. You understand, correct?"

"Of course, but I do hope you'll invite me soon to another hunt. I would enjoy that very much."

"Of course, we would be glad to do that just a little later—maybe in the fall. Not to be rude, but I've guest to attend to. Mr. Sommeren will show you out."

Henry is taken aback by the abrupt end to their conversation but again realizes the culture differences. Henry says his goodbyes, and Mr. Sommeren escorts him back to the gate and out. Henry can't help but think the whole thing was strange, but as long as he gets his money, he guesses that nothing else matters and heads back to Mirror Lake.

Mr. Sommeren goes back to Mr. Amjad and says, "I hope that went as well as we think it did."

Mr. Amjad says, "I believe it did. You have to remember this man is all about money, and he knows nothing about us or our culture, so I think he was fine with what we talked about."

Mr. Sommeren says, "I hope so because we still have a month before we complete what we came to do."

CHAPTER 35

When Henry gets back in Mirror Lake, it's late on Friday night, so he decides to wait until Saturday after lunch to call Gordon. Around 2:00 p.m., he gives Gordon a call.

Gordon answers, "Where the hell have you been? You have been avoiding me. You could have at least called me back. We really need to talk about Chuck and Donald."

About that time, it hits Henry that there was no mention of any intruders by Mr. Amjad, so his little trip didn't yield much. Henry says, "Settle down. I'm sure the boys are all right."

Gordon says in an angry voice, "Don't be so sure. Since you would not call me back, I went and talked with Denton yesterday morning."

Henry says, "Why did you do that before talking with me? I just came back from the hunt club, and everything is all right."

"So you saw Chuck and Donald, and they're okay?"

Henry replies, "No, I didn't see the boys. They were not there, but I did see inside the hunt club, and nothing much has changed. I also spoke with Mr. Amjad, and they have guest there right now, hunting, and they didn't mention having any intruders. Matter of fact, no one could get inside the hunt club unless they wanted them to. They have added quite a bit of security. They have even changed the locks on the gate."

Gordon says, "Well, Denton is really concerned and was pissed I didn't mention knowing the boys the day he put the flyers up. He told me not to tell anyone, not even you."

"Why would he do that and not want me to know?"

"I don't know, but he is going to be mad at me because I told you. So I suggest you and me head over to talk with Denton now."

Henry really does not want to do this but thinks for once Gordon has a point. He really does not want them making such a big deal out of nothing.

Jack Abrams along with several other agents, some from Homeland Security and some from the FBI office in Atlanta, have arrived. They're in Denton's office behind closed doors, going over the information that Jack was able to obtain. They have discovered by using the facial recognition that this Mr. Amjad also goes by Abd al Bari, which in Arabic means servant of Allah and has quite a history of violence. He is actually from Syria, not Istanbul Turkey. He's been underground for a number of years, so not much on him recently and seems to have changed his appearance, as well as his bio. This kept him off the radar, which in its self is scary.

All of a sudden, they hear a commotion at the front desk of the station. Denton excuses himself and goes to see what is going on. It's Henry and Gordon. Henry is arguing with the officer at the front desk. He is demanding to see Denton.

Denton puts up his hand and says, "Okay, quieten down, Henry," and then looks at Gordon with anger on his face.

Gordon says, "I'm sorry. I didn't mean to tell him. It just slipped out."

Denton says to Henry, "Okay, just settle down. I'm too busy to talk with you now, Henry, go back home, and I'll be in touch with you before the day is over."

Henry starts to complained, and Denton raises his voice and says, "Not going to do this now. Again, go home, and I'll call you or come over later."

Henry puffs out his cheeks and turns and leaves. He says to Gordon, "Who does he think he is talking to me that way?"

Gordon says, "That's what I've been trying to tell you. Something big is going on. He's got fellows in his office from Atlanta, and I believe it has to do with our missing boys."

Denton and Jack, along with the other agents, continue to discuss the issue at hand. Jack says he found nothing of importance on Mr. J. Sommeren; however, none of this can be good. He asks

Denton, "What do you know about his dealings with Mirror Lake? I mean, any idea what he is doing here?"

Denton replies, "No, there is no one here that he would be interested in, nor is it close to any military facility."

Jack asks, "What about this property you mention that he leased from your mayor?"

"Well, I really don't know much about it, just that it's up in the northeast corner of the mountains. I do know it's close to the Virginia state line and not all that far from the coast. What are you thinking?"

Jack replies, "Well, what better place to hide and plan another attack. I mean it's only a hop, skip, and jump to Washington. Depending on what their plans are, could it be we are looking at another attack? We certainly can't rule it out. Can we get this mayor over here, so we can find out more about the area, and what we might be looking for?"

Denton calls up to the front desk and asks his sergeant to give Henry and Gordon a call and tell them to get over to his office ASAP. Gordon just happens to still be with Henry, and so they both head back over to Denton's office. Henry says to Gordon, "He better be calling to apologize for the way he talked to me earlier."

Gordon just rolls his eyes; he is really concerned as to what is going on and is really sorry that he is a part of it.

They get to Denton's office and are escorted back to the conference room where Denton and Jack have setup a map and information they have already obtained. Henry walks in and just starts ranting.

Denton says, "Henry, sit down and shut up. We have questions regarding this property you have leased to this Mr. Amjad."

Henry starts to say more, but Denton says in a stern voice, "Sit down."

Henry sits and just stares at Denton with his arms crossed over his chest. Denton says, "Henry and Gordon, this is Jack Abrams. He is with Homeland Security, and these other gentlemen are agents either with Homeland Security or FBI. So I need you to listen and answer any and all questions they have. Starting with where is this property of yours actually located." Henry gets up and walks up to the map and points out where the property lies.

Jack asks, "How many acres are there and are there buildings located within these perimeters?"

Henry says, "There is around three hundred acres, and yes, there are five buildings on the property, some for sleeping quarters and a mess hall and a couple for storage. Why all these question? What is going on?"

Denton says again, "Henry, we will answer your questions later. Now let Jack talk."

Jack says, "Tell me everything you can about this property."

Denton says, "It used to be a hunt club of some kind?"

Henry says, "Yes, for fox hunting but hasn't been used for that in some time. There are only two roads in and out, one on the east end and one at the west end of the property. It's fenced around all three hundred acres. I estimate it to be about six feet tall."

Jack asks, "So why is the whole area fenced in and why six feet high?"

Henry says, "It was prepared for fox hunting and also considering deer as well. For it to be a controlled hunt, it needed to be contained, and the six feet are for the deer. Some of them have high jump capabilities."

Jack says, "So if I'm to understand correctly, it would be very difficult for anyone to get close without being noticed."

Henry replies, "Yes, you are correct. You get in by four-wheel drive, jeep, truck, or four wheelers. Now I demand to know what is going on here."

Jack says, "Henry, Denton here had some reservations regarding Mr. J. Sommeren and Mr. Ameer Amjad, so he asks me to do a background check. After doing this check, we have discovered that Mr. Amjad is a wanted terrorist and goes also by the name Abd al Bari and is a very dangerous man. I, along with my colleagues, am here to figure out what they're doing here."

Henry can't believe what he is hearing and then says, "No, you have this all wrong. These two gentlemen are just businessmen and wanted to be able to enjoy a good controlled hunt while visiting our country. They have some of their friends up there right now, hunting. I was just there yesterday, and I saw nothing strange at all. They just like their privacy because of where they come from."

Jack pulls up some of the info he's gathered on this Abd al Bari aka Mr. Amjad and shows Henry some of his handywork. Henry looks at the info and says nothing.

Gordon looks at Denton and says, "Is this for real?"

Denton says, "Yes, and my guess your boys went in and will never come out."

Gordon looks at Henry and says, "This is serious stuff, Henry, you need to tell them everything you know. You have plats and blueprints of the property and buildings you could give to them. Also tell them about all the added security they have put in place."

Henry just looks shell-shocked.

Denton says, "What kind of security are you talking about?"

Henry says, "They have added razor wire to the top of the fence, and I believe it has been electrified as well. They also put new locks on at least the front gate which is the west-end gate. Also they have guards at the gate."

Denton asks, "Were they armed?"

Henry replies, "I didn't see any weapons."

Jack asks, "Did you look inside any of the buildings?"

Henry replies, "No, I didn't ask to because Mr. Amjad said they had made no changes to the buildings."

Jack says, "Okay, it's late. We can pick this backup tomorrow. We are all tired. Henry, please bring the plats and blueprints here to Denton's office first thing in the morning. Whatever you do, don't talk with anyone about this."

Denton looks at Gordon and Henry both and says, "This means both of you. Do you understand the importance of keeping this quiet?"

Both Henry and Gordon just nod their heads and leave.

CHAPTER 36

That same evening, Denton is talking with Helen, and she asks, "What is going on?" She saw all of the strangers arrive and knew that they were at the station, and she had not heard from Denton all day long.

Denton replies, "A lot, and I'm sorry, but right now, I can't talk about it with you. I wish I could see you tonight. I would love to just hold you in my arms."

Helen says, "Well, I can come over if you want and spend the night."

Denton replies, "I've to be up really early in the morning and back at my office, so I won't ask you to do that tonight. Just talking with you always makes my day better. I'll try to talk with you tomorrow, and maybe by then, I can explain more. I know we haven't really talked about our feelings toward one another, but I want you to know you mean the world to me. Have a good night." Denton hangs up before Helen can even respond. He feels guilty for putting her on the spot like that and really didn't want to get into that kind of conversation over the phone. He knows that whatever is ahead isn't going to be easy. He just hopes whatever it is, they get it figured out in time.

Helen is a little shocked with him ending their call so abruptly; it's not like him. But she feels tingly all over thinking about his comment of her meaning the world to him. She feels the same way and is ready for them to talk about their feelings for each other.

It's Sunday morning, June 2, 6:30 a.m., and Denton is in his office; he's been there since about 4:00 a.m. He couldn't sleep thinking about the implications in what Jack was able to find out about this Mr. Amjad.

Jack knocks on his doorframe, and Denton looks up and says, "Good morning, Jack, hope you rested better than I did last night!"

Jack replies, "Probably not, but I'm ready for us to see what our options are as far as this so-called hunt club property is concerned and what they're doing there. You can bet it isn't hunting. The other agents should be here by 7:00 a.m. They just stopped by for a bite of breakfast. Have you heard from your mayor yet?"

Denton replies, "No, but I'll get my officer at the front desk to give him a call telling him to get here by 7:00 a.m. and make sure he brings copies of the plats and blueprints of all buildings with him." Denton then calls his officer at the front desk, asking him to call Henry at home and remind him to bring the plats and blueprints. Denton then continues his conversation with Jack, "He should also be able to tell us about all trails or off-road ways of getting closer to the property. Jack, what do you think we are looking at here?"

"I'm not sure but given this guy, Abd al Bari's history, it can't be good. Problem is there are a number of targets north of this so-called hunt club that would be easy access from there. You've got the Naval Station Norfolk, Langley Airforce Base, the Pentagon, and of course, the White House just to name a few. What I'm interested in is seeing what avenues of travel closest to this property is available to them for transport of any means for an attack and best getaway routes they might take. Maybe this will help us narrow down what target they might have in their sights."

The other agents have now arrived, and they have begun going over their information once again, throwing out there their thoughts and different scenario's they can come up with. About 7:20 a.m., Henry and Gordon arrive, and Henry has brought the plats showing all roads and other areas surrounding the property known as the hunt club. Also he's brought the blueprints for the five buildings within the property perimeters. This will help them see all roads and most of the trails or other ways in which this property may be approached. Of course, things have changed over the years, but hopefully Henry and/or Gordon can fill in any blanks.

As they're going through this new information, especially the plats for the property and comparing them with a more current map, Jack ask Henry, "Exactly what did you see when you were up there on Friday?"

Henry says with a bit of tone, "I told you already what I saw, and it all looked legit."

Denton says to Henry, "Okay, Henry, lose the attitude. We need your help here. We don't need you fighting us all the way."

Gordon steps in and says, "Listen, Henry, I know the money we got is important, but nothing is more important than figuring out if these guys are up to no good, and also we owe it to Chuck and Donald to find out what has happened to them. So answer their questions and cooperate here. Don't make this harder than it has to be."

Henry looks a little red-faced and says to Jack, "Okay, what is it you want to know that I haven't already told you?"

Jack says, "Just close your eyes and think about what you saw as you approached the hunt club."

Henry replies, "Well, I went in by the road approaching the west-end gate to the hunt club. I didn't see anything out of the ordinary until I got to the gate. There were guards at the gate."

Jack stops him there and asks, "Were they armed?"

Henry replies, "No, they didn't have weapons at least any that I saw. They were just standing there, and also now that I think about it, that Mr. Sommeren was standing there. It was a bit odd. It was as though he was waiting for me."

Jack interrupts, "Like he knew you were coming?"

Henry replies, "Yes, like he knew I was coming. Once on the inside of the gate, I was looking around and noticed the changes to the fence and the gate. You know...the added security. Mr. Sommeren walked me to the building where Mr. Amjad was waiting. I mentioned looking around, and he said that they had guest there that was from another country, and that they didn't like outsiders intruding on their hunt. I also mention the added security, and he said it was for their guest that they were from another country where it was required, so he just obliged them this. He then ended our conversation before I could really say anything else and walked out. Mr. Sommeren escorted me to the gate as though not asking just telling me it was time for me to go."

Denton looks at Jack, and they both say at the same time, "They have spotters."

Jack finishes his thought, "Or camera's around the compound." Jack then turns to Henry again and asks, "Did you see anything mounted on the fence, poles, or the buildings that looked like cameras?"

Henry replies, "No, but I really didn't notice that sort of thing they could have had them. I'm just not sure."

Jack nods at Denton, then Denton asks Gordon, "Gordon, do you have anything you want to add to what Henry has said here today?"

Gordon says, "No, I haven't been up there since they took over, so there isn't anything more for me to tell you other than I'll do anything I can to help just let me know."

Denton says to both men, "Thanks, Henry, for bringing the plats and blueprints and for giving us the information we have ask for, and, Gordon, thanks for coming forward with this. Now both of you go home and go about your business as usual. Don't talk about this to anyone. You understand?"

Both men just shake their heads and leave.

Henry looks at Gordon and says, "Do you think this is for real? I mean this sound serious."

Gordon says, "Yes, I think it's serious, and I believe that they have done something with Chuck and Donald. I just hope they're not dead because if they are, it's on us."

Henry says, "Well, we didn't know that these guys were bad, so we didn't do anything on purpose."

Gordon says, "That doesn't matter. It still is our fault if something has happened to them. Let's just hope they find them all right."

Both men go their separate ways for the rest of the day.

CHAPTER 37

Jack looks at Denton and says, "What do you think about all of this? Do you think Henry is being up-front with us about what he knows?"

Denton says, "Yes, I do. I know Henry is all about money, but I know he also loves his country. I don't think he had a clue as to what these men are truly about. He just saw an opportunity to make some money and went with it."

Jack says, "I believe you are right. This Mr. Amjad did his homework where Henry is concerned and this area as well. He saw an opportunity to use Henry, and it appears to have worked out well for him. I just hope we can figure out what they're up to, and that it leads to their plans, so we have time to stop them before they can act on anything."

Denton has a thought and says to Jack, "You know they had artwork shipped into Atlanta from Turkey. I believe that was then shipped up here to our Mirror Lake Arts and Antiquities Gallery for show and for sale. I know Helen Coleman, the owner of the gallery, maybe we should talk with her and also her sister, Margaret."

Jack says, "What does her sister have to do with anything?"

Denton says, "Mr. Sommeren and Mr. Amjad are clients of hers and the firm she works for in Atlanta Gilpin, Grays and Connor Financial Group. They came to this financial group for help with investments, and Margaret was given them as her clients. She was the one that introduced them to Helen and the gallery."

Jack says, "Before we talk to either of them, I need to run a background check on this financial group to see what kind of ties they might have with the Middle East."

Denton says, "I don't think you'll find anything, but I understand the need to first check them out. You do what you need to do, and then I'll ask Helen to contact Margaret and have her drive up here, so we can talk with both of them together."

Jack says, "That sounds like a plan, give me until tomorrow afternoon, and we will talk again. I should know more by then, and maybe we can talk with them on Tuesday sometime."

Denton says, "Okay, you can work here from my office if you like or go back to your room at the resort."

"I think I'll go back to the resort and work from there. That way, I can work with the agents from the FBI as well, and we can do what checking we need to on both sides. I'll let you know what I come up with, and we will go from there."

"That's fine. I need to do some other work for a while. We will talk tomorrow then."

Jack leaves, and Denton works on some paperwork and thinks about talking with Helen.

That afternoon, Denton gives Helen a call. When Helen answers, he says, "Hi there, are you busy? Can you talk?"

Helen says, "Sure, I can talk. I was just reading a book. Are you okay? You sound very tired?"

Denton says, "I'm tried, and I would really like to see you. Do you think you can come out to my place tonight for a while?"

Helen says, "Sure, you want me to bring some food? I think we have plenty leftovers from Sunday's lunch, that's if you like roast beef, potatoes, and carrots?"

Denton replies, "That sounds great. I haven't had a good meal in days, and I'm hungry, not just for food, but for you as well."

Helen laughs, and then Denton says, "I'm sorry that didn't come out right. I just really miss you and need to talk with you, so let's say around six-thirty. Is that okay?"

Helen says, "Perfect. See you then."

Helen gets to Denton's right at six-thirty. She's really missed him and is ready to spend time with him. He meets her at the door and takes the food from her hands, and they go into the kitchen where he sets the food down and turns and takes her in his arms and kisses her. As the kiss grows deeper, she moans. He takes her in his arms and goes back to his bedroom. They spend several hours in each other's arms, making sweet love without ever speaking a word. It's a moment in time neither one of them will ever forget. They both realize that they will never be the same again.

It has gotten dark outside, and Denton looks into Helen's eyes and kisses her lightly and says with a smile, "I'm starving."

Helen laughs and says, "Me to."

They both get up and pull on their clothes and go into the kitchen. Helen warms them both a plate of food, and they sit at the table and start talking. Helen asks Denton, "Can you talk about what is going on now?"

Denton replies, "Actually yes, I need to talk with you about what is going on."

Helen's eyebrows rise just a little, and Denton continues, "Remember when I mentioned to you about talking with a friend with Homeland Security a few days ago?"

Helen nods.

Denton says, "Well, he did some checking on this Mr. Sommeren and Mr. Amjad and found out that Mr. Amjad, also known as Abd al Bari, is a known terrorist."

Helen says, "Really? So is that why all these strange men are in Mirror Lake?"

Denton says, "Yes, one of them is my friend, Jack Abrams, with Homeland Security. He has other agents with him from Homeland Security, as well as from the FBI office in Atlanta. We don't know what these guys are up to yet but know that it can't be good. We have already talked with Henry and Gordon regarding property that Henry leased to these men up in the northeast corner of the mountains. Henry says that they're just using it for controlled fox hunts, but Jack believes otherwise. And given the history of this Mr. Amjad, I understand why."

Helen asks, "Why wasn't this Mr. Amjad on a watch list and caught before entering into the US?"

Denton replies, "Well, he's apparently been underground for some time and not only changed his bio, but his appearance as well.

So he was able to appear as a legitimate businessman since he was with this Mr. Sommeren, whom Jack found to at least appear legit, then no questions asked."

Helen says, "So what does this all mean? Where do I fit into all of this since I've been doing business with them?"

Denton replies, "Well, we want to talk with you and Margaret about that—"

Before Denton could continue, Helen interrupts, "What does Margaret have to do with this?"

Denton says, "Well, they're her clients."

Before Helen could say anything more, Denton holds up his hands and says, "Don't worry, we all know neither of you have anything to do with this. After Jack does a quick background check on Margaret's firm to make sure they don't have other contacts or clients in the Middle East, then Jack, along with me, will talk with you and Margaret both."

Helen says, "Well, I don't think they will find anything on her firm that will look bad, but I still don't follow what they're looking for from us."

Denton says, "Just thinking about the art's shipment that came into Atlanta, and what might have come in with it."

"Oh, I didn't think about that, and Margaret and I really never talked about it. I don't think Margaret ever saw it. She just made arrangements for it to be shipped from Atlanta to Mirror Lake. And once it arrived here, I was the only one at first that was here in the gallery when I opened it. There was nothing out of the ordinary with it or on the shipping manifest."

"Most likely there was nothing more to it. But it could have been an avenue in which they used to smuggle something into the US using the art as cover. Please don't talk to Margaret about this before you hear from me on Monday."

"Okay, but are you planning to go to Atlanta to talk with her, or do you want her to come here?"

Denton replies, "We want her to come here, but I'll let you know on Monday. That way, it will give her enough time to drive up on Tuesday."

"Okay, I promise I'll not talk with her until I hear from you."

"That was a great meal. I can't tell you how much I enjoyed it."

Helen smiles and says, "Thanks. Are you ready for a little more desert?"

Denton smiles, and they both get up and go back to the bedroom. It was the best night either of them had in a very long time. They never really talked about their feelings for one another, but it was obvious to both they felt the same way.

CHAPTER 38

Early Monday morning, June 3, Denton and Helen are in his kitchen, having coffee and breakfast. Denton looks at Helen and says, "Last night was amazing."

Helen looks at him with a smile and says, "Yes, it was. I don't think life gets any better than that."

Denton says, "You are right. I thought I could never feel this way again, but I believe this is even better if that's possible."

Helen blushes and says, "I feel the same way, but I know there is a lot going on right now. We both know that we are here for each other no matter what, but I believe other than stealing time for ourselves once in a while, we have to put this on hold until the situation you have is resolved. Don't you agree?"

Denton replies, "Yes, I know you are right, but I'm really going to have a hard time not having you in my arms every available moment. But I do realize that the next week or so is going to be hell. So I agree, but hopefully we will be able to see each other at least long enough to steal a kiss. I guess we need to get going. I need to be at the office in less than five minutes."

Helen laughs. "I don't think you are going to make it."

Denton says, "Oh well, they can get started without me."

They get their things together and leave.

Denton gets to his office and greats the officer at the front desk and asks if he has any messages. The officer tells him no there are no messages. He goes into his office and gives Jack a call to see how things are going and to see if he's got any more information regarding the situation.

Jack answers his phone, "Good morning, Denton, did you rest better last night?"

Denton replies, "Let's just say a different kind of rest. How about you?"

Jack replies, "Yeah, I rested. Stayed up a little later then I planned. The boys and I got to talking about our situation here and started throwing out different ways to approach this property, but I have to say nothing sounds good. I'm afraid that these fellows chose well when choosing this property because it's inapproachable. I don't even think drones will work here either, too many trees and foliage."

"I was afraid of that. We are going to have to have someone that really knows these woods and can get in and out without being noticed for any recon. I've been thinking about that as well, and I might have an idea. Let me do some checking, and we will talk later today about it, okay? I also wanted to know if you have had time to run the background check on that financial group that Margaret works for."

Jack replies, "I've sent the info into our office, and they're doing it now. Haven't heard back yet. It might take a couple of hours before I hear something. As soon as I do, I'll let you know so you can have this Ms. Coleman contact her sister and have her drive up tomorrow morning."

"Sounds good. I'll be here in the office, working. Let me know if you need anything or when you hear back on any of these things. I'll talk with you later this afternoon."

"Sounds good. Later."

Denton recalls back to when Helen was doing the renovations on the gallery and to a conversation he had with Billy Bob. Billy Bob was the contractor Helen was using for the renovations. They were talking about hunting and all of the good places north and northeast of Mirror Lake there where to hunt deer. Billy Bob had told him that any time he wanted to go hunting to let him know, and he would take him; he had also mention some fellows that were just over the Virginia state line that he went hunting with from time to time, and they were really good at picking up the scent of deer and also not being able to be spotted by the deer so as not to spook them off.

Denton calls Helen at the gallery to see about getting Billy Bob's number. He rings Helen's number. Helen answers, "Well, hello, I really didn't expect to hear from you this soon. Everything okay?"

Denton replies, "Yeah, I just need something from you. Do you have Billy Bob's number with you?"

Helen says, "Yes, do you need some work done?"

Denton laughs at the way she says this and then replies, "No, I just want to talk with him about the mountains up in the northeast corner of the state. I was remembering a conversation we had while he was still working on the gallery."

"Oh, okay, give me just a minute." While she is looking for Billy Bob's number, she asks Denton, "Have you heard anything about the background check yet on Margaret's firm?"

Denton replies, "No, not yet, it may take several hours. But as soon as I hear something, I'll give you a call. That way Margaret can come up tonight or in the morning?"

"Okay that sounds good, and here is Billy Bob's phone number, 828-657-1212."

"Thanks, and I'll talk with you later today, but it will be after lunch sometime."

Denton gives Billy Bob a call. When Billy Bob answers, Denton says, "Hello, Billy, this is Denton Gage, the sheriff of Mirror Lake. Is it okay if I call you Billy?"

Billy Bob replies, "Sure, what can I do for you, Sheriff?"

"We met through Helen Coleman when you were working on the renovations for the gallery, and we talked about deer hunting up in the northeast corner of the state. Do you remember that?"

"Yeah, I remember you and the conversation. Are you looking to go hunting sometime? You know deer season isn't until the fall?"

Denton says, "Yeah, I know. I just need to talk with you about the northeast corner of the mountains. Do you have some time to spare today to come into my office and talk for just a little while?"

"Sure, I'm actually doing some work on a friend's house just outside of Mirror Lake, and I could be at your office say around 4:00 p.m. this afternoon, will that do?"

"That will be just fine, and I really appreciate it. Thanks. See you then."

"Sure, don't mind at all. See you then."

114

CHAPTER 39

It's around 2:30 p.m. on Monday, June the third, and Denton is working at his desk when his phone rings. Denton says, "Denton here, what can I do for you?"

Jack replies, "Denton, it's me, Jack, and I've the report back on the financial firm in Atlanta. It's coming up clean. So you can let Ms. Coleman know she can contact her sister and ask her to come up to Mirror Lake and meet with me and you tomorrow. Let's say around 2:00 p.m."

Denton says, "Sure thing, I'll do that as soon as we get off the phone. But since I've got you on the phone now, what are you doing this afternoon at about 4:00 p.m.?"

Jack says, "Just same thing I'm doing now, going through this stuff over and over again. Why? You need something?"

"Yeah, I need you to come over to my office at around 4:00 p.m. to meet with a fellow that I believe may be able to help us out as far as getting close enough to this property to see what is going on. At least it's worth a shot talking with him."

"Okay, see you at 4:00 p.m. this afternoon."

Denton gives Helen a call.

Helen answers, "Hi again, do you have some news for me?"

Denton says, "Yes, Margaret's firm came up clean, so do you mind giving her a call and asking if she will drive up tonight or in the morning for a meeting at 2:00 p.m. tomorrow?"

Helen replies, "No, I don't mind, and she will probably come tonight if I can get hold of her now, and she has no meetings late today. I'll try to talk with you tonight. I know you are busy, but you know you can call me anytime day or night."

Denton thinks how much he loves this woman even though he hasn't said the words yet. He replies, "I promise I will and thanks for being so understanding."

Helen says, "How could I not be? I mean this is my hometown and my country. It all means the world to me as so do you. Talk later."

Helen hangs up and almost cries; she so much wants to say the words *I love you*, but she isn't sure he is quite ready to hear them yet.

Helen gives Margaret a call, and when Margaret picks up, Helen says, "Hi, sis, are you busy? Can you talk?"

Margaret is worried because Helen does not usually call during the day, and she sounds a little off. Margaret responds, "Sure, for you, anything. But I've got to ask, is everything okay up there? Are you okay?"

Helen replies, "Yeah, I just need you to come up tonight if you are not too busy to get away quick enough."

"Yes, of course, I'll come tonight. I've no meetings lined up. I was going to meet some friends for an after-work cocktail, but I can do that another time. You sure everything is okay up there?"

"Yes, I need you here for a meeting tomorrow afternoon around 2:00 p.m., but we really need to talk first, so if you get up here tonight then that will give us plenty of time for talking without disturbing mom."

"Sure, I'll do my best to be on the road between 4:00 and 4:30 p.m. this afternoon. So I should be there no later than 8:00 p.m. tonight. If it looks like I'm going to be much later, I'll give you a call."

"Sounds good. Talk when you get here, just be careful."

Denton is in his office when Jack arrives at quarter to four; he looks up as Jack is walking in and says, "Hi there, you look a little haggard."

Jack replies, "No shit!"

Denton laughs and says, "Sorry, have you found out anything more that can help this situation?"

Jack replies, "No, not really, I'm hoping that what I hear in this meeting will shed some light on which way to go with this. Thanks by the way for pitching in on this and trying to find a way around this mess we have uncovered."

"No thanks necessary. You know how I feel about all these bastards trying to do harm on our soil. I never intend to have to face what we did on 9/11 ever again."

Jack says, "I understand how you feel at least in part. We are going to stop this, Denton, whatever it takes. I promise you this. On a little different topic, were you able to contact—sorry—what were their names again?"

Denton smiles. "You talking about the sisters?"

Jack laughs. "Yeah, I'm sorry I've looked at so many names on this that I can't keep them straight."

"That's okay. The owner of the gallery is Helen Coleman, and her sister is Margaret O'Keefe. She works for the financial group in Atlanta. And yes, Margaret will be coming up most likely tonight."

Jack asks, "Where does she stay when she is in town?"

Denton replies, "She stays at her mother's, which is where Helen lives as well."

Jack looks at Denton with a grin and says, "You seem to know a lot about these two woman. Do I detect a little more than just an acquaintance here? And if so, which of the two do you know the best?"

Denton laughs and says, "Okay, you got me there. I've been seeing Helen for a little while now. I didn't say anything because I didn't want to mix work with pleasure and didn't think it matter to the case. I still don't think it matters to the case, but I do realize we need to look at every avenue. Not that I think that either of these woman have any terrorist connection, but since they somewhat know these two gentlemen, I understand the need to talk with them."

Jack says, "Good. I know you would never do anything to jeopardize the situation, and I'm actually glad to hear you are moving on with your life. You know Jenny would want you to."

CHAPTER 40

Just about that time, the officer at the front desk buzzes Denton's phone to let him know that Billy Bob Johnson is here. Denton tells him to send him back. Denton meets Billy at his door and shakes his hand and says, "Thanks for coming. I really appreciate this."

Billy responds, "Well, you kind a have my curiosity up. I didn't think you were asking me here to talk just about hunting."

"You are right. Please come in and sit down. I want to introduce you to Jack Abrams. He is with Homeland Security and will be joining in on this conversation. Jack, this is Billy Bob Johnson."

Jack rises and shakes Billy's hand and says, "Nice to meet you. Sorry, it's under these circumstances."

Billy walks in and sits down and looks at Denton with questions written all over his face. Before he can say anything, Denton says, "Jack, I haven't told Billy actually why he is here yet, just that I wanted to talk with him about the northeast corner of the state."

"My bad. I'll shut up now and let you talk, Denton."

Denton looks at Billy and says, "What I'm about to tell you, you can't talk with anyone else about, understood?"

Billy replies, "Understood. But can I say you are scaring me just a little here."

"Don't mean to, but this is very important and very high profile. We have come across some information that leads us to believe that we have a possible terrorist group on some property up in the upper northeast corner of the state. It's property that was once used as a controlled fox hunt club. Do you know this property?"

"Sure, I think everyone around here knows about that property. I believe it belongs to Mayor Mason, at least it once did."

"You are right. It still belongs to Henry Mason. He, just a few months ago, leased it to two gentlemen from the Middle East, a Mr. J. Sommeren and a Mr. Ameer Amjad for a year. Supposedly they're going to use it for controlled fox hunting. However, we have found out that this Mr. Amjad is a known terrorist named Abd al Bari. This man is very dangerous. We need some Intel on the property and are trying to find the best way to get it. We already know that it's near impossible to get to and observe by land or air without them knowing about it. That's where you come in, at least we hope. We even have the plat of the land and the blueprints for the five buildings on the property."

Billy looks a little strange in color but says, "Sure, anything I can do to help. I'm all yours."

"Thanks. We can't begin to tell you how much we appreciate your cooperation and help." Denton looks at Jack and says, "Okay, take it away. I assume you have already thought about what questions you need answers to."

Jack says, "Yes, I have. As Denton says, we have looked at these plats and talked with Henry Mason regarding the lay of the land surrounding this so-called hunt club, which we need help navigating. This is where you come in. We hope you can help us with this. Denton says you hunt a lot and had mentioned knowing this land very well."

Before Jack could continue, Billy kind of holds up his hand and says, "Okay, I understand what you are saying, but don't you have Special Forces that can do this kind of recon for you that would be better equipped than someone like me?"

Jack looks at Denton and back at Billy and says, "Yes, son, we do, and we are not asking you to do the recon. We are just asking for help in making sure our approach will be the best possible approach available. Now is that clearer for you?"

Billy smiles and says, "Yes, sir, sorry. I was just not sure what you were expecting out of me. Don't misunderstand, I'm willing to do anything I can to help. It's just that I'm limited in training. I was in the military for a while, but my training is limited at best.

However, I'm good with tracking and an excellent marksman. So let's get started."

Denton pulls out the plat he's got and a current map and says, "Let's go to the conference room so we can spread this out and talk about what we are looking at."

They take the plat and map and go to the conference room and spread it out on the conference table and start going over everything. Denton has a red marker and hands it to Billy, and Jack starts with the questions as Billy marks places on the map and puts remarks in the margin. They stay at this until 7:00 p.m. when they finally come up for air, and Jack says, "I think we just might have a plan. What I want to do is get the group that will be doing our recon in here by Wednesday, June 5, and go over this with them. Billy, do you think you can come back in and meet with them as well?"

Billy answers, "Sure, not a problem, this kind of makes me think I'm back in the military. Don't want to call it fun because of the situation but brings back memories."

Jack asks, "What branch were you in, and if I might ask, why did you leave the service?"

Billy is quiet for just a second then says, "I was a marine helicopter pilot for medivac mostly. I was deployed in Operation Desert Shield better known as the first Gulf War. Most people have no clue as to what went on over there. It was a mess even though they claimed it to be a victory and an easy one at that, which was not the case. Let's just say, I saw things I'll never be able to get out of my head and leave it at that. I served just short of seven years in the marines. I thought it would be my home until I retired, but things happen that change a man. I decided not to stay in the marines. Understand something, it had nothing to do with love for my country or the marine corp. I just decided I wanted to come home to my first home and make a life with someone that would love me and accept me as I'm."

Denton and Jack just look at each other and nod. They totally understand where this young man is coming from. They both think to themselves that they didn't go wrong by choosing to bring this man into the situation here. Denton says, "Thanks so much, Billy, and again I can't stress the importance of not talking about this with anyone. I'll give you a call either tomorrow or Wednesday morning to let you know when we will need you to come in again for the next meeting. I know this is a bit overwhelming but try not to worry about it. We plan to have this situation under control and stop what these guys have planned in time to really celebrate the fourth of July in style."

Billy shakes hands with Denton and Jack and leaves. Jack looks at Denton and says, "That was a good call on your part, bring Billy in. I think he will be a great help with forming the best plan we can have. I was very impressed with him."

Denton says, "Yeah, me too. I had a good feeling about him when I first met him."

Jack asks, "How did you meet him?"

Denton replies, "He is a contractor and did the renovations on the gallery Helen owns."

Jack smiles and says, "Well, I guess I better get back to the resort and start making some calls. Catch you later."

Denton says, "Yeah, later."

CHAPTER 41

Denton decides before leaving his office to give Helen a call. She answers, "Hi there, how has your day been?"

Denton replies, "Better now that I hear your voice."

"Mine as well. But really, how did your day go? Any better today? Any more information?"

"Well, Jack and I met with Billy Bob, and he is helping us understand the area around this so-called hunt club. Did you know that Billy was once in the marine corps?"

Helen replies, "I knew he was in the military, but that's about it. He is a lot younger than me. His military days were during the timeframe I lived in South Georgia. So you think he can help out with this situation?"

Denton answers, "Yes, I do. He is a very bright young man and has a lot of military background, along with knowing this property, makes it a great plus."

Helen says, "I'm glad you reached out to him. I know Billy is a good man and will be more than willing to help in any way possible. I might not know much about his military background, but I know a lot about his character, and it speaks volumes."

"Yeah, I could tell that when I first met him when he was working on the gallery. He seems more than eager to help us with this situation. Now how was your day?"

Helen laughs and says, "A little uneventful, but I spoke with Margaret, and she will be here by 8:00 p.m. tonight."

"Good. Do you girls want to meet for a late dinner?"

Helen answers, "Well, not sure. I know she is going to want to talk about this situation, and why you want to talk to both of us. So

I'm thinking it will be better for her to come straight to mother's and talk without you around."

"Ouch, that hurts!"

Helen laughs. "You'll get over it, and I'm pretty sure she will go back to Atlanta tomorrow, so if you are not working tomorrow night, then I'll come out to your place and kiss your ouch."

Denton replies, "Now that sounds like a good deal to me. But you know, this ouch is getting bigger by the minute. So by tomorrow night, it might just cover my entire body."

Helen laughs. "Well, I'll make sure my lips are ready for that, and I promise that you'll forget all about your little ouch."

They both laugh and hang up, and Denton heads over to the resort to have dinner with Jack and the guys, and Helen heads home.

Denton gets over to the resort and calls up to Jack's room and asks, "Have you had dinner yet?"

Jack replies, "No, I haven't. I thought you would be having dinner with your lady friend."

"I talked with Helen, but her sister, Margaret, is coming in tonight, and they want to talk, so I'm eating alone unless you want to join me."

"Yeah, I'm hungry. What do you suggest?"

"There is this little café called Maddie's Café, and it has great food. Come on down, and we'll walk over since it's a nice night. Do any of the other guys want to come with you?"

"No, they all went to a neighboring town for some seafood. I'll be right down, and this will give us a chance to talk."

*****

Margaret gets to her mother's just a little before 8:00 p.m. and is really glad to be there. The drive up was not as soothing as usual because of all the things that were running through her mind. She just couldn't imagine what was going on. She walks into the kitchen, and Helen is there to greet her. They hug, and Helen says, "Was your drive up okay?"

Margaret replies, "Well, it was uneventful, but I had all kinds of things running through my mind, so I need you to enlighten me."

"Sure thing, but first, mother is still up in the den. She would not go to bed before talking with you, and of course, she wanted to be sure you got here okay."

They go into the den and sit and talk for about twenty minutes, and then their mother says goodnight and heads off to bed. Margaret looks at Helen. "Okay, start talking."

Helen says, "Well, Denton has had some uneasy feelings regarding Mr. Sommeren and Mr. Amjad from the onset, but he didn't know actually why. He's got this friend with Homeland Security, so he had him run a background check, along with photo facial recognition on both of these gentlemen and found out that Mr. Amjad is a known terrorist by the name Abd al Bari and is very dangerous."

Margaret can't believe what she is hearing, so she stops Helen right there and says, "Are you serious? They really think these two men are terrorist?"

Helen replies, "Yes, they don't just think they know. Also this Mr. Amjad has leased some property from Henry Mason up in the northeast corner of the state, and they believe they have a group of terrorist that are there with them, and they're not sure what they're up to. But they're sure of one thing, they're not hunting. On top of that, there are two young boys that Henry Mason hired to go up there and snoop around, and now they're missing. Denton is afraid they may be dead."

Margaret just sits there with her hand to her mouth; she can't believe what she is hearing. She then asks, "Okay, so why do they want to talk to us. They don't believe we have anything to do with this, do they?"

"No, they don't. They have questions regarding the art shipment we received. I told Denton I didn't think you even saw the shipment that it came into Atlanta, and you had it shipped directly to Mirror Lake. That's correct, isn't it?"

"Yes, you are correct. There was no need for me to inspect the shipment, so I just gave the shipping information to shippers, and that was that. You didn't see anything funny with the shipment once it arrived in Mirror Lake, did you?"

"No, and I've already explained this to Denton. They may want to know who did the shipping from the start until it arrived up here just to talk with them as well, but I don't believe you, or I've anything else to contribute. So nothing to worry about. I'm just worried about what they're going to find and just how bad it is, and of course, I'm really worried about Denton."

Margaret asks, "Speaking of, how are things going with you two?"

"Great. I really like him. Actually I think I'm in love with him."

Margaret smiles and says, "I knew it. I just knew. Have you told him you love him?"

"No, at least I haven't said the actual words *I love you* yet, but he and I both know that's where this is going. I just worry that this situation is going to bring up bad memories for him, and I'm not sure what they might do to him, especially where I'm concerned. And I know that there isn't anything I can do about it short of being there for him and making sure he knows that."

Margret gets up and hugs her sister very tightly and whispers in her ear, "Everything will be all right. You both will get through it together."

They both just sit there and hug and cry together. Then they go to bed and try to get some sleep.

Helen's phone rings about 11:30 p.m., and she sees it's Denton. "Hi there, is everything okay?"

Denton replies, "Yeah, I just got home, and I hope I didn't wake you, but I just needed to hear your voice, and I wanted to know if Margaret got there okay?"

"Yeah, she got here just fine, and we talked. She is a little worried about what you guys are thinking about me and her and our dealings with Mr. Sommeren and Mr. Amjad, but I told her there was nothing for her to worry about."

"You are right, and this may be a waste of time, but you might find you know something without even realizing it. That happens sometimes, and we need every bit of information we can get to take these men down. I won't keep you up any longer. I'll see both of you tomorrow at 2:00 p.m. in my office."

"Yes, we will be there."

Denton is quiet for just a few minutes then says, "Helen, I love you, just wanted you to know." He hangs up the phone before Helen can say a word. She lies there in bed and just cries she loves him to.

CHAPTER 42

It's Tuesday, June the fourth, and Denton is back in his office at 6:30 a.m. He is looking over the mail from yesterday and thinking about what is on his plate for today. He was to meet with the chamber of commerce today, regarding the fourth of July celebrations to go over security and anything else that falls under his jurisdiction. But he's already let them know that he will not be available today but will send over one of his officers to fill in for him. He knows that this will be a very busy day—actually the rest of the week will be busier than he's seen since relocating to Mirror Lake.

*****

Henry Mason is just having breakfast when his phone rings, and it's Gordon Grover. When Henry answers, Gordon says, "Henry, have you heard anything from Denton or this fellow from Homeland Security?"

Henry replies, "Good morning to you too, Gordon."

Gordon replies, "Sorry. Good morning. I'm just a little nervous about all of this that's going on, and I don't like not knowing what is happening."

"You need to quit worrying. We have done nothing wrong. So no matter what happens, we are in the clear."

"Nothing's wrong? What about Chuck and Donald? They were our responsibility, and if something has happened to them, what would you call that?"

"Unfortunate. That's what I would call that. However, we don't know if anything has happened to them. As far as we know, they never went up to the hunt club. So let's not make something out of nothing yet, okay?"

"Well, I wish I could be more like you and have no feelings at all, but I'm sorry, I can't do that. These boys didn't do anything to deserve to die or anything else. They were just out to get a little money and beer and have some fun."

"Again, we don't even know if they went up there, let alone know if they're dead. So stop all of this morbid behavior and move on until we have something to really worry about. But even if something has happened to them, we had no idea what they were walking into, so it's still not our fault if, and that's a big if something has happened to them."

Gordon was just silent on the other end for just a moment or two and then says, "You know, you are a real piece of work, Henry—all about the money."

Henry, with anger in his voice, says, "Well, I don't remember you turning any of your portion of the money down now, do I."

Gordon just hangs up on Henry. Henry sits at his breakfast table and just stews over this whole situation.

*****

It's now 1:30 p.m., and Denton hasn't moved much since he got into his office, other than refilling his coffee cup multiple times. Jack appears in his door way and says, "Good afternoon, Denton, are you thinking or just napping with your eyes open?"

Denton laughs. "Well, a little of both I think. Not actually napping but maybe daydreaming?"

"Oh, really? And what pray tell were you daydreaming about? Could it be about a little woman by the name of Helen?"

Denton with a smile on his face. "Maybe. If it were, it was the best part of my day so far."

Jack laughs. "Okay, I get the drift you had rather daydream about Helen any day than see my ugly mug, right?"

"Hands down, Helen would win every time."

They both just laugh, and Jack comes on in and sits down. He says, "Are we ready for what today brings?"

"Yeah, might as well be. It's coming whether we want it to or not. But maybe we can get a handle on this and get moving with whatever plan we need to end this thing before it really begins."

*****

Helen and Margaret are just leaving their mother's home, headed into town to Denton's office. Helen says, "Are you ready for this?"

Margaret says, "As ready as I'll ever be. I know we haven't anything to worry about, but it's scary just the same."

"I know I'm scared as well. But I know Denton believes in us, and I may not know this friend of his, Jack, but I know Denton will take care of us. So no worries."

Margaret says, "No worries. Agreed."

They get to Denton's office a little early, and the officer at the front desk just sends them back. Denton meets them at his door and introduces them to Jack, and they all go back to the conference room. Denton asks them, "Can I get you anything to drink?"

They both respond with a no thanks.

Denton says, "Let's begin. Jack, I'll turn it over to you for any questions you might have."

Jack says, "Thanks, and again, ladies, I want to thank you both for coming in. It's greatly appreciated. Mrs. O'Keefe—"

Margaret stops him right there and says, "Please call me Margaret, and it's Ms. not Mrs…"

Jack smiles. "Okay, Margaret it is. You work for the financial group, Gilpin, Grays and Connor in Atlanta, correct?"

Margaret replies, "Yes, I do. I've worked for them since 1982."

"And this Mr. J. Sommeren and Mr. Ameer Amjad came to Gilpin, Grays and Connor looking for help with investments in and around the South East?"

"Yes, they did… Well, as far as I know, they did talk with one of our partners, Mr. Andy Gilpin first, and he assigned them to me. I'm one of the senior financial advisors with the firm."

"So are there any other investments that you presented them with that they have made investments in anywhere up the eastern coastline."

"No, not that I'm aware of. I gave them a number of choices in and around the metro Atlanta area, anything from restaurants, commercial, to even several residential developments to consider. But I also included my sister's gallery because I thought that it would be good for her and them as well. They seemed very excited about that. Mr. Sommeren, who was the only one I really met with before the galleries opening, said that Mr. Amjad would really be pleased with the gallery because he loves art and would really like to introduce their culture through their art, and what better way to do that than through an art gallery. And I think, at least somewhere in the back of my mind, he seemed to know something about Mirror Lake."

"Really? Did he say they were familiar with Mirror Lake already?"

"No, it was just a feeling I got that they knew something about the resort."

Jack says, "Okay, now I understand they had a rather large shipment of art shipped into Atlanta headed to Mirror Lake. Is that correct?"

"Yes, it is, but I had no need to view or go over this shipment while it was in Atlanta. I just made the arrangements for it to be shipped straight to Mirror Lake."

"Do you know how it was shipped and where it first arrived into the US?"

"Yes, it arrived via ship and came into the harbor in Savannah, then shipped by ground to Atlanta. Then I made the arrangements for it to be shipped by ground to Mirror Lake. I had nothing to do with the shipment or arrangements until it reach Atlanta."

"I see. Who did you use for the shipment to Mirror Lake?"

"I used UPS. That's who we use for all of our shipments."

"I think that's all the questions I've got for you, Margaret. But can you get me information on who and where the shipment begin until it reached Atlanta where you took over?"

"Yes, I'll see what I can get for you and get back to you as soon as possible."

Jack then turns to Helen. "Hi, Helen, I feel like I already know you. Denton speaks highly of you."

Helen blushes a little. "Thanks. He's told me a little about you as well. It's nice to meet you, however, not under these circumstances."

"I agree, but I do have just a few questions for you if you don't mind."

"Of course not, whatever you need, I'm here to help."

"I understand that the shipment arrived at the gallery, and you were they only person at the gallery when it arrived?"

"Yes, I was. I have a small staff, and most of the time, they're just part-time. I received the shipment and started opening the boxes and comparing the items with the manifest received with them. Also I had a list of the inventory, which Margaret provided, of what was to be in this shipment and used it as well to compare to the manifest also."

"Was there anything strange or missing about this shipment?"

"No, everything that was in the shipment was on the manifest and also on my inventory list. Nothing was out of place or missing."

Jack turned to Margaret. "Where did you get this inventory list from?"

Margaret says, "From Mr. Sommeren. I had asked for it before the shipment arrived so I could give it to Helen. She used it to help with setting up the gallery for opening night."

"Well, ladies, I think that's about it, and, Margaret, if you can get me that information as soon as possible and get it back to me, or you can fax it to Denton, and he will make sure I get it, and I think we are done. Again, I can't thank you enough for coming in, and Margaret, especially you for driving all the way from Atlanta to Mirror Lake to meet with me."

Margaret says, "It was my pleasure. I'm sorry for all of the trouble that seems to have arrived on the heels of this investment and these clients of mine, but hope you guys can get it all sorted out and taken care of."

Helen looks at Denton and says, "You need anything else from us before we go? I think Margaret is going to head back to Atlanta as soon as we are done here."

Margaret says, "Yes, I need to get back for some very important clients that I'm meeting with tomorrow, but I'll get the info you need first, Jack, and send it to Denton."

Denton says, "That's great, and no, I believe we are done here. Again thanks, ladies, and Helen I'll talk with you later this afternoon."

Helen just smiles and nods, and they all get up, shake hands with Jack, and say their goodbyes.

CHAPTER 43

It's now a quarter to four and about time for Jack and Denton's meeting with Billy. Helen and Margaret have just left, and Denton turns to Jack and says, "Want some coffee?"

Jack says, "Yeah, I'm so tired. I think I need a whole pot."

They both go to the break room and get coffee and a stale donut and go back to Denton's office. They haven't even had time to finish the donut when the officer at the front desk buzzes back to Denton's office and says Billy Bob is here. Denton tells him to send him on back. Billy walks into Denton's office and says, "Good afternoon, gentlemen, you both look a little like zombies."

Jack says, "We feel a little like zombies. Would you like a cup of coffee? The other guys haven't gotten here yet but should be here any minute. We had them stay in a motel not too far away, so it would make it easier to keep this whole thing under warps as long as possible."

Billy says, "No, thanks on the coffee, and I understand we have a lot of nosy people around here, and they love to gossip, don't they, Denton?"

Denton responds, "Yeah, I've got a glimpse of that just a little. But I'm sure it's like most small towns, and they seem to thrive on gossip."

About that time, the officer at the front desk just walks in with the guys from Special Forces, and Denton and Jack stand along with Billy, and Denton says, "Okay, let's all go to the conference room." Denton turns and says to the officer, "We need more chairs please in the conference room. Can you take care of that?"

The officer just says, "Sure, be there in just a few."

There are about six guys that just came in. They include one coordinator and five Special Forces guys. They only need three other chairs, and the officer brings in two then goes back for the third. Now they're all in the conference room, and Denton asks, "Would anyone like something to drink? We have sodas, water, and coffee."

They chime in all at once and say water. Denton thinks that makes it easy and turns to the officer and asks him to bring in bottles of water.

Jack says, "Okay, let's all sit and get started by doing introductions."

Jack starts the introductions with "this is Denton Gage, the sheriff of Mirror Lake, and this is Billy Bob Johnson, who has a great background in the military and knows the property in question very well. And I believe most of you know me, I'm Jack Abrams with Homeland Security. Now how about going around the table and just giving your first names."

The coordinator stands up and gives his name first, "I'm John," and then turns to the next guy. "This is Al, Josh, Milton, Wallace, and Tommy."

Jack says, "I believe you all have been briefed on the situation before coming up here so you have a good idea what we are looking at. What we hope to gain today is a plan to do recon on this camp better known around here as a hunt club. What we know now is that it's very limited on ways in and out. There are a lot of woods and very dense foliage, which makes it near impossible to observe from the air. We are certain that this is a terrorist group because of one of the main persons in this so-called hunt club, which we will refer to as the camp, is a known badass named Abd al Bari. He's been underground for a long time, so not much on him at present. But his past history speaks for itself. So just his presence here lets us know that there isn't anything legit about this so-called hunt club. Billy, as I said before, has a great working knowledge of how the military works and is very familiar with this property, so I'm going to turn the floor over to him. Feel free to ask questions anytime."

Jack nods at Billy. Billy stands and goes to the map so he can better show the area and talk about what he knows and thinks. They go over every inch of the property, and Billy tells them how he see it, and they ask questions so to understand what they're looking at.

By 7:00 p.m., they feel they have a plan that will work. But before they leave, Billy looks at Denton. "I've one more thing I want to bring up, and now is as good a time as any."

Denton says, "Go head," then looks at Jack and shrugs.

Billy continues, "Okay, once you have done your recon and know what you are looking at—by this, I mean how many combatants you are looking at and their arsenal—you are most likely going to need more men than just the five of you guys in this room here. Now I know of a group located just over the Virginia state line that are what you would call a little unconventional, but what I call good guys that love this country. Most of them have some military background, and all they want is to keep our country safe. And what they have that you'll need is more firepower and better knowledge of the area and ways to get in and out before anyone knows they're there." Billy looks at Denton and Jack and says before either of them can speak, "No, I haven't talked to them about this situation at all. I just know that they can be of great help once you all are ready to move. We all know that in a situation like we have here, it has to be quick and quiet. So what are your thoughts on this before I go to them and bring them in?"

Denton looks at Jack, and Jack says, "Well, Billy, I, for one, trust you very much, but let me and Denton and John here talk it over before you go forward, okay?"

Billy says, "That sounds good to me, just let me know when and give me a time to have them here, or if you feel a need to meet somewhere a little more private, I can arrange something not that far out of town."

Denton says, "That sounds good. We will be in touch tomorrow again. Thanks, Billy."

Everyone says goodbye, then Jack says to John, "Hold back just a minute please."

John nods and tells the others to wait outside; he will be right out. Jack, John, and Denton talk briefly regarding what Billy has said, and they agree to bring these guys in and also to meeting somewhere outside of town. Denton tells them he will speak with Billy and make sure where they meet will be secure first and will talk with Jack tomorrow morning so they can meet again tomorrow afternoon. They all agree they have to get what Intel they need as soon as possible because they have no idea what these guys have planned or when they plan to execute, so no time to waste.

CHAPTER 44

Everyone has gone now, so Denton gives Billy a call. Billy answers, "Billy here."

Denton says, "Billy, it's me, Denton. Jack, John, and I talked about this and agree on bringing in these guys you are talking about. I just have a few questions for you. First, do you know all of these guys personally and were any of them dishonorably discharged from the military?"

Billy replies, "Yes, I know them all and have known them most of my life. All of our fathers grew up together and all love the sport of hunting. Most of them have military background, and no one has ever been dishonorably discharged. Matter of fact, most of them spent more than five years in the military. They're just like me. We are all around the same age and saw some form of combat. We all kind of got tired of the politics playing a major role in arears they had no business in."

"Okay, I understand where you are coming from, and I've a lot of faith in you and your judgment, Billy, and I do believe you are right. In that, we are going to need all the help we can get. We don't want this thing to go sideways on us and innocent people get hurt. And I think that if we don't do this right, there is a good possibility of that happening. Okay, now what about this place you are talking about us meeting at tomorrow?"

"It's my place. It isn't huge, but I built it myself, and it has one large living space. We can move my things out of the way, and I already have a large table and can get more chairs or other means of ways to sit. I think it will work well, and I'm located way out in the woods, so no one to snoop."

Denton thinks to himself, *I really like this boy; he reminds me of a younger me,* then says, "That sounds good, Billy, you go ahead and contact these guys and let's set this up for 2:00 p.m. tomorrow afternoon. I need directions to your place."

Billy gives Denton the directions he needs, and then they say their goodbyes. Denton calls Jack.

Jack answers, "Hi, Denton, what's up?"

"I just got off the phone with Billy. All I can say is I love that boy. This group of guys he is talking about he grew up with, and most of them have military background with at least five years' experience in the military and no dishonorable discharges."

Jack says, "That sounds great. Did you go ahead and set up this meeting?"

"Yes, it will be tomorrow at 2:00 p.m., and we are meeting at Billy's place. I've got the directions. You guys just meet me here about 1:30 p.m."

Jack says, "Sounds like a plan to me. I've got a good feeling about this. For once, the good guys are going to rule. Have a goodnight, Denton."

Denton says, "You too. See you tomorrow."

Denton then gives Helen a call at the gallery, and she answers, "Hi, how are you? You still walking around?"

Denton says, "Yeah, a little tired but a lot stoked."

Helen smiles. "So something went well today, I take it."

"Yeah, I would say so, and again I sure am glad you used Billy Bob Johnson to do your work on the gallery. He is definitely a gem in the rough."

"Well, I guess that worked well for both of us, right? Now are you working tonight?"

Denton, with a smile on his face, says, "No, I'm not. So are you saying Margaret went home, so you are free tonight for a little ouch kissing?"

Helen says while trying not to laugh, "Sorry, but Margaret is still here. The ouch kissing will have to wait."

Denton makes a sound she's never heard and says, "Well, I sure needed some ouch kissing tonight, but I guess if I have to wait, I just have to wait."

Helen just burst into laughter, and Denton says, "Okay, I'm going to get you for that. So what time will you be at my place tonight?"

Helen looks at the clock on her desk and replies, "Well, it's about 6:00 p.m., and I need to run home first. I'll be out there about seven-thirty. Is that okay? But I'll not spend the night because I know you have a busy day, and I might stay at home a while tomorrow before going into the gallery."

"Is everything okay at home with your mom?"

"Yeah, she is just a little under the weather, and given her age, I worry about her, so I'm going to spend some time with her tomorrow and maybe take her to the doctor if she will go."

"Okay. See you at seven-thirty, and I'll have us something to eat. Be careful."

Helen gets to Denton's a little before seven-thirty, and they sit out on the back porch and have dinner and talk. Denton tells her all about what went on for the last several days and tells her tomorrow will be a turning point. He hopes by Friday or Saturday at the latest they will be ready to take these men down. He really wants to see an end to this before they have a chance to carry out whatever it is they have planned. Helen understands but can't help but worry about all of this. It's so close to home. She thinks what if they have a nuclear bomb, even if it isn't big, it could still do a lot of damage to North Carolina, but she doesn't want to ask in part because she doesn't want to know the answer.

Denton says, "Okay, enough shoptalk. I believe you owe me a little ouch kissing."

Helen forgets the bad thoughts she was having and laughs out loud. "Well, I never go back on a bet or a promise, so where do you want this ouch kissing to start, and I don't mean what part of your body, where in the house or out here," then she smiles, and Denton takes her in his arms and not another word is said.

CHAPTER 45

It's Wednesday, June 5, and Denton is in his office dealing with everyday business. It's about twelve noon, and Helen appears in his doorway. Denton looks up and grins, and Helen says, "How you doing this morning? Did you get some rest last night after I left?"

Denton smiles and says, "Slept like a baby. How about you? What are you doing here? I thought you were going to spend time with your mom today?"

"Well, I had breakfast with her, and she seemed better, and of course, didn't want to go to the doctor, so I decided to come in, and I thought you might like some lunch. So I stopped at Maddie's and brought something. And yes, I slept wonderfully."

Denton says, "You know I think you just might be a keeper. I'm starved. I didn't bother with breakfast this morning, just have had coffee."

"I was afraid of that, so stop what you are doing and let's go to the conference room and eat."

Denton gets up and follows Helen to the conference room, and they talk while they eat their lunch.

Once they have finish eating, Helen throws away the papers their sandwiches were in, and Denton walks over and takes her in his arms and gives her a kiss that lingers. Once he stops, she just looks into his eyes and says, "I love you."

Denton says, "I love you too."

Denton then releases her, and they walk out together, and Denton tells her he will call her sometime later, might be after 8:00 p.m. tonight.

Helen smiles and says, "Stay safe, and I'll wait for your call." Helen leaves the station and heads to the gallery. She knows she has to stay busy in order to not think about what is happening in their little state of North Carolina.

It's now 1:30 p.m., and Jack and the guys from Special Forces have arrived and are waiting on Denton in the station parking lot. Denton comes out and gets into the vehicle with Jack and John. Al, Josh, Milton, Wallace, and Tommy follow in the second vehicle. It doesn't take long for them to get to Billy's place, but he was right. It's way off the road back in the woods, and if you didn't know it was there, you would never see it. There were several vehicles already there, so they all pile out and go to the door. It opens before they can knock, and Billy is there. He says, "Please come in, and we can do some introductions and get this party started."

Denton leads the way; the rest follow, and once inside, Denton can't believe how large the room really is. Billy has already pushed his things back against the wall and had the table set up in the middle of the room, and he already had about eight chairs and had pulled in several homemade chairs out of stumps and branches. Then he also had several just large stumps that could be used like stools. There was more than enough for the fourteen people that made up this unusual group.

Billy says, "Grab a chair or stool and have a seat around the table. As you see, I already have a current map, and Denton provided me with the plat and blueprints. Would anyone like something to drink?"

They all shook their heads no and started making their way around the table.

Denton says, "Billy, I really want to thank you for this, and I'll start the introductions if that's okay."

Billy says, "Sure, go right ahead once you are done. I'll introduce our little group."

"Okay, I'm Denton Gage, the sheriff of Mirror Lake. This here is Jack Abrams with Homeland Security, and with him is John— sorry, guys, I'm just going with first names here—who is the coordinator for Special Forces, and his team, Al, Josh, Milton, Wallace, and Tommy."

Billy says, "Thanks, Denton. Now this is Jason, Paul, Robby, Stanley, and Peter. We all grew up together. Our fathers were friends and were big hunting buddies. Most of these guys have had military experience, so we all are great with tracking and using rifles. I might add that we are all excellent marksman."

Denton says, "Thanks, Billy, and I also want to say thanks to you guys as well. I know Billy has briefed you on what we are doing here and what we are looking at. If it's what we think it is, it'll be no walk in the park."

They all nod in acknowledgment to what Denton has said. Then they get down to business. They go over everything that Denton and Jack, along with John and the guys, went over the day before. Billy and the others were able to add to what they already know.

By late that afternoon, they had a plan worked out. Two of the Special Forces guys, Al and Tommy, along with Jason and Robby, are going to do the recon. They're going to start out tonight after dark. Once they have done their recon—which will also consist of some technology that the Special Forces has, using inferred to show how many bodies are in the compound—they will come back and meet at Billy's again on Thursday and work toward finalizing their plans. Denton and Jack head back to Mirror Lake, and John along with Josh, Milton, and Wallace head to their motel for the night. They plan to meet back at Denton's office by 9:30 a.m. on Thursday, June 6, and head back out to Billy's to go over what Al, Tommy, Jason, and Robby were able to find out. Hopefully it will give them everything they need to take down this cell and prevent whatever it is they have planned.

Denton and Jack talk about everything on their way back to Mirror Lake, and one of their biggest concerns is what type of weapons or possible bombs they have there at this site. They realize a lot depends on what their target is. There could even be chemical weapons there on site, and there will be no way of knowing. Jack agrees with Denton on their approach as far as using the Special Forces and Billy, along with his guys, but he can't help but think they need stand by backup, especially for possible chemical weapons. He tells Denton he is going to talk with the FBI guys back at Mirror Lake; he has no choice but to update them and will ask about what is available from the Atlanta FBI office as far as possible chemical weapons are concerned. He tells Denton he will have this information ready for tomorrow's meeting, and then he drops Denton off at his office.

It's now right at 8:00 p.m., and Denton decides to call Helen before he heads home. He dials her number, and Helen answers, "I'm glad to hear your voice. Are you okay?"

Denton says, "Yeah, just tired. I would love to see you, but I'll have to be satisfied with just talking tonight."

Helen realizes he really sounds down but instead of talking about what has gone on today, she decides to keep it upbeat and says, "So you love me, do yah?"

Denton, with a smile on his face, says, "Yes, ma'am, I reckon I do."

They both laugh and talk just a little longer, mostly about nothing. They say their good nights and hang up.

CHAPTER 46

It's Thursday, June 6, and it's 9:00 a.m., and Denton is in his office, and Jack walks in. Denton says, "How you doing this morning? Any sleep last night?"

Jack says, "Yeah, a little, but you know how it is when you have people out in the field, you sleep with one eye open."

"Yeah, I remember those days and even though they're not my guys, I have to admit I was the same way. So I assume you have heard nothing?"

"You assume correctly, but I look at that as good news. I hope they're at Billy's, catching a little shut-eye."

"Well, I guess we will know here soon. John and the others should be here any minute, and we will head on out to Billy's—" Denton no more than got that sentence out when John and his guys walked in; they're ready to go. They all go out. Jack and Denton take Denton's truck. and John, Josh, Milton. and Wallace pile back in John's SUV and follow Denton once again to Billy's.

They get to Billy's about 9:45 a.m., and Billy meets them at the door. They go inside and right away find that Al, Tommy, Jason, and Robby haven't returned as of yet. This causes concern all around. They had expected them to be back to Billy's by around 4:00 a.m. Billy lets them know that he hasn't heard anything, and that they haven't tried to contact them because of the possibility of giving them away. They're standing around talking about what to do next, especially if they don't hear from them within the next two hours when they walk in the door, looking a little haggard but still all in one piece.

They drop their gear and ask for coffee, then they all sit around Billy's table once again to go over what they have learned. They explained why it took so long; it was not easy getting even close to the camp. They told them they have claymores all around the compound fence, which is six feet then another twelve to sixteen inches in razor wire, and it's also electrified. They're also six men outside the fenced area as spotters. They also have cameras all around inside the compound. Some of these are pointed toward the fence. They were able to get close enough to use the inferred equipment to determine how many bodies were inside the compound, and they have at least a good estimate of around twenty people, and maneuvering the claymores took a lot of time.

The other problem is there was no way to determine what kind of weapons they have other than the automatic rifles the men were carrying outside the fence. Jack says, "Okay, so we know for sure this is no hunting club, and that it's definitely tied to terrorist. So any suggestion as to what our next move should be?"

John looks at his guys, and Jason speaks up, "Well, I really don't see a way into that compound without just being captured by these guys and taken into the compound. But even if someone did that, then there would be no way to get information back out. So my best suggestion is to take what we have and plan our assault based on that."

Jack looks at John and asks, "John, do you think that's our best assessment of the situation?"

John says, "Yes, I'm afraid it is. Jason here is the best threat assessment guy we have and if I say, a damn good one."

They all kind of nod to each other and then get down to business.

Denton says, "I know that I don't have the extensive military background that the rest of you have, however, could it work if we go in around predawn hours and where the fence is most vulnerable, disarm the claymores and if possible, cut through the fence, gaining access into the compound. That's if we have means of cutting through an electrified fence?"

John says, "Actually we do have a means of cutting through an electrified fence, or I should say some electrified fences? Jason, do you think this fence will work with our equipment and allow us to cut through it successfully?"

Jason says, "It's a good possibility, but I didn't have time to look at how they have this setup. But being that, it's so far out into the wilderness. Yes, there is a great possibility for this to work."

Denton says, "Okay, let's says we can get into the compound. There are fourteen of us, and you feel certain there is, let's say between sixteen to twenty men inside the compound and at least six men outside the fence. Do you believe our fourteen can handle at least twenty-six combatants?"

John says, "Well, what we would have to do is systematically take out the six men outside the fence before cutting into the fence and entering the compound? If we can do this quickly and quietly, then yes, I believe we can do this. I know that my five guys have this capability."

Billy speaks up, "The six of us also have this capability, so if we handle the six guys outside the fence, and we do them all at the same time so no chance of them setting off any kind of an alarm and your guys cutting the fence, then we can join you, and all enter the compound at the same time. That certainly levels the playing field."

Denton says, "You also have to remember that this Mr. Sommeren and Mr. Amjad, which I'm assuming are making up part of the bodies inside the compound, most likely are not armed the same as the others."

Jack says, "I've also arranged for backup from the FBI office in Atlanta, just in case they have bombs setup or chemical weapons. So if we needed extra firepower, then they would be close by. Also we can use the four FBI guys that are already at Mirror Lake."

John asks, "Any feedback from anyone or other suggestions?"

No one spoke up with any other suggestions. Denton says, "Okay, sounds like we have a plan. Now how soon can we go forward with this plan. I can't say exactly why I have this feeling, but I believe we are running out of time here. So today's Thursday, June 6, so do you think we could pull this off either Saturday or Sunday?"

Jack says, "I know that looking at Sunday as the attach date gives us enough time to make sure we have our backup in place, so that part is covered. John, how do you feel about your guys and the equipment you need to do this?"

John says, "No problem. We already have our equipment and are ready to go."

Denton says, "Billy, how do you and your guys feel about this? You ready to do this by Sunday?"

Billy looks around at his guys, and they all nod, and he answers, "Hell, sir, we are ready to do this right now and feel with this plan, we can be successful."

Denton says, "Well then, I say we are a go. So for the next two days, get plenty of rest, check all your gear, and let's be at Billy's no later than 2:00 a.m., Sunday morning, ready to implement this plan around 4:00 a.m., Sunday morning, June the ninth at our destination. Okay, we need to make sure we all have at least Kevlar vest and any other protection gear for this assault."

John says, "My guys have everything we need but no extra."

Jack says, "He has some with him and knows that the FBI guys do as well. I can check on getting more if we need them for Billy's guys."

Denton says, "I only have three vest in my office, but we can use those as well. Jack and I'll do a count and see what if any others we need."

They all feel this is a good working plan, and they head back to Mirror Lake.

CHAPTER 47

Mr. Sommeren and Mr. Amjad are in the compound, talking about what has gone on for the last couple of days. Mr. Sommeren is still concerned that given Henry Mason's appearance at the compound unannounced could still cause problems. He thinks that Mr. Amjad is underestimating this man's potential for being a problem for them. He thinks they should move the attack date up to June 15, just to be on the safe side. After all, they're ready to go now. They have the bomb already loaded on the truck for the attack on the west end of the National Mall of Washington, and the chemicals are loaded into light bulbs and safely secured in three backpacks that will be walked into to the east end of the National Mall of Washington. This will effectively cause the most chaos and damage possible. Of course, they most likely will sustain causalities as well, but their men are prepared to sacrifice their lives for the cause of Allah. Mr. Amjad is still adamant that he will not change the date from July 4 to June 15. He's given up too much already, making the change from September 11 to July 4. Mr. Sommeren realizes there is no talking with him regarding any more changes. It does not relieve his sense of urgency however.

Henry is sitting in the G&G Bar and Grill on Thursday night, talking with Gordon. Henry is still pissed because he doesn't know what is going on. He or Gordon neither one has talked with Denton. He can't believe his luck with things. But Gordon keeps reminding him that they already have the $300,000. So no matter what happens, that money is theirs. Henry agrees he is just greedy enough that he wants the money for the second-year contract as well. Plus, he was excited about being able to rub elbows with more men who were at least as wealthy as Mr. Amjad or possibly more.

Denton and Jack head over the G&G Bar and Grill for a night cap. Denton has already talked with Helen about what has gone on today. They made no plans to see each other, but Helen thinks she will surprise him and be at his place when he gets home. She realizes it might be late because he had mentioned having a drink with Jack. But she decides it will be good for him and equally as good for her.

As soon as Denton and Jack walk into the G&G Bar and Grill, Henry seizes the moment and walks right up to Denton and in a loud voice says, "Denton, I demand to be updated on the situation that's going on in Mirror Lake."

Denton grabs Henry by the arm and promptly walks him out of the bar. Henry is still speaking in a loud voice, but luckily, he is drunk enough that no one can understand what he is saying. Jack gets them a table, and Gordon comes over and says, "Sorry about that. He's been drinking all afternoon. When he gets this way, there is no talking to him."

Jack asks, "He hasn't been spouting off his mouth in here, has he? Because if he has, that could be a problem for us."

Gordon replies, "No, he hasn't, just to me. I've been able to keep it down so far."

Jack says, "That's good because you never know who is around to hear something that can create a real problem for us."

Meanwhile, Denton has Henry out by his car and is trying to get him to quiet down. Finally, Henry shuts up long enough for Denton to speak and actually be heard. Denton says, "Henry, if you don't stay sober and quiet, I'm going to lock you up for at least a week. Do you understand me?"

Henry, in an angry voice, says, "You'll do no such thing. I can fire you whenever I want. Remember, I'm your boss."

Denton says, "You can do whatever you want to me in another week or two. But right now, you'll do as I say, or I'll lock you up. Do you understand me? And as far as what is going on here right now, you don't need to know. Just know that it's a big deal, and you don't need to be involved. Now you have two choices here, you can go home and stay there at least until next Monday, June 10, or I can lock you up. What's your pleasure?"

CHAPTER 48

Denton and Jack have had a couple of drinks while talking about Henry. Denton talks with Gorgon as well and tells him to do his best to keep Henry out of town. He explains to Gordon the situation is hopefully going to come to an end within the next five days, and they don't need problems out of Henry. Gordon lets Denton know he fully understands and will do his best to keep Henry under wraps and away from town. Denton thanks him for his cooperation and understanding. Gordon just nods and goes back to work. Denton and Jack go their separate ways, and Denton heads home.

When Denton gets to his house, he notices a light on in his living room and thinks to himself he doesn't remember leaving it on. However, it was still dark outside when he left for work this morning. He walks into the house and see's Helen lying on his sofa asleep, and he grins. He walks over and bows down to give her a light kiss on the lips. Helen opens her eyes and smiles up at him then puts her arms around his neck, and he lowers himself down to kiss her more. He is surprised but very happy she is there. She can make the worse day in the world a little lighter.

She sits up, and he sits beside her on the sofa; he just starts talking. He tells about meeting Billy's guys and how impressed he is with them. Also tells her about the Special Forces guys and how ready they are to take this terrorist group down. He knows he can tell her anything, and it will go no further than her ears. He lets her know about their plans to move on this early Sunday morning, and hopefully it will all be over by noon on Sunday, June 9.

She listens to everything he is saying and is really worried about what could happen but knows that everyone involved is very equipped to handle whatever happens. But she can't help but worry about all of them, especially Denton. Helen thinks to herself that she never expected to find love again and was okay with that, but now that she has; she doesn't want anything to take that away from her.

They talk until around 2:00 a.m., and Helen says, "I really should go." Denton by this time has hold of her hand and looks into her eyes and says, "Please stay. All I want to do is hold you in my arms and never let you go. You have no idea what you mean to me and what a calming affect you have on me. You really bring me peace."

Helen looks into his eye with tears in hers. "I love you to and if anything happened to you, I don't think I could survive."

"You don't have to worry. We have everything under control. Let's go to bed and get some sleep. It will be okay for me to go in a little late in the morning if you can."

"Yeah. I let mother know where I was going to be. I mean she already knows about us, and she really loves you."

It's Friday morning. Helen and Denton are in his kitchen, fixing breakfast when Denton's phone rings. Denton answers, "Denton here, what can I do for you?"

It's one of Denton's officers, and he has Gordon in his office. He is telling him that Gordon is concerned because he went out to Henry's to check on him this morning, and Henry was not there. The officer also tells him that Henry's car is no longer in the parking lot at the bar. Denton asks, "Does Gordon know where he could have gone?"

The officer tells him no. Denton says, "I'll be there in about forty-five minutes. Tell Gordon to check Henry's office if he hasn't already done so and then meet me back at my office in an hour."

They hang up, and Denton tells Helen what went on last night at the bar with Henry and what he had to do. So now he is worried about what Henry is trying to do. Helen says, "Well, let's finish and get you into the office as soon as possible."

Denton gets to his office around 10:00 a.m. on Friday, June 7, and finds out that Henry had called a meeting with the board of commissioners and is planning to try and get Denton fired. Denton can't believe Henry but realizes maybe this is a good thing. He contacts

Jack Abrams and informs him of the situation. Jack comes right on over to Denton's office to go with him to this meeting to help explain what the situation is. Hopefully this will get Henry off Denton's back and at the same time keep him quiet.

Denton and Jack get to the town hall for this meeting at twelve noon. They walk in, and everyone is there, and of course, Henry is already up to his old tricks. They call the meeting to order, and Denton gets up to explain the situation to the board. Denton says, "First and foremost, I would like to introduce Jack Abrams, who is with Homeland Security out of Washington DC."

Jack stands and says, "Good afternoon, gentlemen, I'm here in support of this situation that your sheriff Denton Gage is here to tell you about."

Denton takes over as Jack sits down. "I know that you all are not aware of what is going on in our state of North Carolina, let alone our town Mirror Lake—"

Henry starts to interrupt Denton when the commission chairman tells him to sit down and shut up. He then tells Denton to continue. Denton says, "Thanks. I believe you all were at our new art gallery opening a while back, and mostly saw or met the two gentlemen from the Middle East, who has some art from their area showing at the gallery. I was a bit concerned when I met these two men that night and started doing some checking on them. That's where Mr. Abrams with Homeland Security comes in. He did some back-checks on this Mr. Sommeren and Mr. Amjad and found that Mr. Amjad is a known terrorist by the name of Abd al Bari and is a very dangerous man. Also I'm sure you are not aware that Henry Mason leased some property that he owns up in the northeast corner of the state to this Mr. Amjad."

They all turned and looked at Henry with a stern look on their faces. Denton continues, "Now you have to understand that Henry here knew nothing about this gentleman or his dealings, just that he was someone looking for investments and wanted a place to hunt with privacy. So Henry didn't do anything wrong, but this does not change the situation at hand. I and Jack here, along with a group from the FBI office out of Atlanta and a group of Special Forces guys, have been working on a plan to defuse the situation here. This is all I can afford to speak of because of the nature of this issue. I hope you can understand and leave me to the task at hand. Once this has been resolved if you feel the need to have another meeting and to terminate me, of course, that's your prerogative."

The chairman of commissioners says, "There will be no need for that. We hired you to protect and serve. As I see it, you are doing your job. Please forgive us for this inquiry, and we will leave you to resolve this situation. Henry will give you no more problems."

Denton says, "Also you need to realize the importance of keeping this quiet. What we have talked about today can't leave this room."

They all agreed, and the meeting was adjourned.

Denton and Jack leave the hall and go back to Denton's office. Once back in his office, Jack says, "Well, at least your board of commissioners is sane."

They both laugh, and Jack heads back to the resort.

CHAPTER 49

Helen is at the gallery, working on putting more things out, even some of the inventory from Mr. Sommeren and Mr. Amjad. She wasn't sure if she should in light of the situation; however, these items are some of the ones for display only. Also business for the gallery has really picked up for the summer. Mirror Lake has really grown into a true tourist attraction. Helen has summer help, but she needs to stay busy and having someplace to go is really good for her. Plus, she really loves working with art and being able to talk to the customers about the history is just icing on the cake. She can't help but think of Denton and wondering what is going on. She knew that he was having issues with Henry. No surprise there, Henry can be a really big pain in the behind. She decides to give him a call.

Denton answers, "I was just thinking about calling you. Jack and I are about to head over to Maddie's for lunch. Would you like to join us?"

Helen says, "Yes, I would and if you can talk, you can tell me what went on with this issue with Henry."

"Sure, we will see you in about five or ten?"

"Good. I'm headed out the door as we speak."

Denton and Jack are already at a table when Helen walks in. They both stand as Helen reaches the table. Denton pulls out her chair, and Helen sits. Denton says, "I'm glad you could join us. You already know Jack."

Helen nods to Jack and says, "Good afternoon, Jack, good to see you."

Jack says, "You too, and I'm equally glad you could join us for lunch. It's always nice to look at a pretty face instead of always having to look at Denton's mug."

They all laugh a little, and the waitress comes over and takes their order. Once she's left, Helen looks at Denton and says, "You okay? What kind of trouble has Henry been trying to stir up?"

Denton says, "Yeah, I'm okay. He just call a meeting of the board of commissioners and was trying to get me fired. He isn't happy that I haven't included him in on what we are dealing with right now. But there isn't anything he can help us with, and he doesn't need to know any more than he does now. Gordon is trying to keep him away, but he is a slippery little devil."

Jack says, "Good thing you have a sane board of commissioners. It didn't take long for them to put Henry in his place. They were more than willing to let Denton here take care of this situation for them. The less they know, the better they like it."

Helen says, "I'm sure you are correct about that. They have no clue, and they don't want to know. All they want is someone to take care of it for them. And they're smart enough to know that they have that in Denton."

Their food arrives, and they began eating with less talking. Once they have finished their meal, they say their goodbyes, and Denton tells Helen he will call her later. Helen heads back to the gallery. Denton and Jack head back to his office. Jack says to Denton, "I can understand what you see in Helen, not only is she a looker but is very intelligent as well. What I don't understand is what she sees in a mug like yours." Jack laughs out loud and slaps Denton on the back.

Denton replies, "Okay, now there isn't anything wrong with my mug, and I really have a way with the ladies. But all kidding aside, she is a really terrific lady, and I'm extremely fond of her. Actually that's not correct, I'm in love with her."

"Really? I'm glad for you. You deserve someone good in your life, and she seems to fit the bill. But I've one question or maybe two. Does she know how you feel, and does she feel the same way?"

Denton says, "Yes, she does. She actually loves me. We are moving kind of slow, but we have both admitted that we love each other.

Not sure what is going to come next. I've been so tied up with this issue that we really haven't had that much time to talk about what we want for the future, but we will. As soon as this mess is over, we will have lots of time. Because most of the time, our little town of Mirror Lake is very quiet."

CHAPTER 50

It's 6:30 p.m. on Friday, June 7, and Denton is ready to go home. He calls Helen to see where she is.

Helen answers, "Hi, are you headed home?"

Denton says, "Yeah, just wondering what you are doing. Have you left the gallery?"

"Yes, I'm at home, and I've fixed dinner for mother, but I was hoping you would call, and maybe we could have dinner together."

Denton smiles. "I was thinking the same thing. Do you think you could come out to my place and stay the night. I mean we can spend the biggest part of the day tomorrow together. I've got to meet Jack, John, Billy, and the rest of the guys by 4:00 p.m. at my office to go over things, and we most likely will not sleep again until all of this is over. We have to leave Mirror Lake no later than 2:00 a.m., Sunday morning, in order to be at the compound no later than 4:00 a.m. Hopefully it will all be over by 7:00 a.m., Sunday morning."

"I don't even like to think about what you all are about to face. It really scares me. I know you have done a lot to prepare, but I also know there is no way for you to prepare for what they have inside that compound. You may know how many men are there but no way to know what kind of weaponry."

"I know, but we have a really good group of men and committed to this task and very well trained. Plus, we will have backup not that far away for any help with special situations as far as any bombs or chemical weaponry is concerned. Now would you like for me to cook us a steak? I'm prepared for that, and you can just come on out, and once we have eaten, we can go sit by the lake and watch the sun set."

"That sounds wonderful. I'll be there by seven-thirty. See you soon."

Helen gets to Denton's a little before seven-thirty, and he is on the back porch, watching over the steaks. He's already prepared a salad and baked potatoes. He looks up and says, "Hi there, just in time, these are about to come off the grill, so just have a seat and pour yourself some lemonade or grab a beer out of the cooler."

Helen pours herself a glass of lemonade and sits at the table. She sees Denton has already set the table, so there isn't anything for her to do. Denton takes up the steaks, and they sit together and eat.

Once they're through, Helen starts to clean off the table, but Denton stops her and says, "Leave that be, let's go down to the lake and wait for the sun to set."

Helen takes his hand, and they take the path to the lake to their favorite spot and sit in the swing that Denton has put up in the last several weeks. It's a beautiful night, and they just sit and watch the sun sets, holding hands, not saying a word.

Once the sun's set, they head back to the house, and each grabs something from the table and takes into the house. They clean up together, and then they go into the den and begin talking. Helen looks at Denton, "Are you ready to talk about what we said to each other a couple of days ago, or is it too soon?"

Denton says, "You mean what we finally put into words that we love each other?"

Helen smiles. "Yes, that would be the thing I'm talking about. Those three little words *I love you*. I know that both of us have loved in the past and have pain from those loves. I also know that there was nothing that either of us could do to stop what happened in our lives or change it. But are you ready to move forward? Because if you need more time, I can understand. I mean my issue was very different from yours. Doesn't take anything away from my grief, but yours was a different kind of tragedy."

"I'm not going to lie to you. I loved my wife, Jenny, more than life itself. But you are right, I had nothing to do with what happened, and there was nor isn't anything I can do to change it. I've already told you that I never expected to ever fall in love again, and I had resigned myself to that. But I can also tell you that I fell in love with you the very first time I saw you. It just took me a while to admit it."

Helen, with tears stinging her eyes, puts her arms around Denton's neck and pulls him to her. They kiss for a long time then get up and head back to the bedroom; no other words needed.

It's Saturday morning, June the eight. Denton and Helen are in the kitchen, preparing breakfast. Denton looks at Helen. "How do you feel about taking a little hike around the lake this morning after we have our breakfast?"

Helen says, "That sounds great. I brought some good shoes and have shorts to wear. Do you have any bug spray?"

"Yeah, somewhere around here, I should have some."

Helen laughs, and they finish eating and dress and head out for their hike.

Once they're back at the cabin, it's around 2:00 p.m., and they sit on the front porch and talk about all kinds of things in their lives that they love. Sharing with one another their likes and dislikes before they know it, it's 3:05 p.m., and Denton says, "I need to shower and change."

Helen says, "Go ahead, I'll wait here for you. Just a quick question, do you have everything you need already together for this mission?"

"Yeah, it's all at my office, so nothing else I need to do short of showering and dressing." Denton comes back out around three-thirty, dressed in dark camouflage and says, "I guess I need to head back to the office." He pulls Helen into his arms and kisses her hard and long and whispers in her ear, "I love you."

Helen says with tears in her eyes, "I love you too, and I'll kill you if anything happens to you, understand? By the way, I like the look. It's a good look for you."

Denton grins. "I promise nothing will happen to me. We will be back here on Sunday night, doing the same thing, okay?"

Helen isn't able to speak, just nods and heads to her car.

CHAPTER 51

Denton gets to his office about 3:50 p.m., and Jack is already there. Denton says, "Hey, you okay? Need something or just needed a little time to yourself?"

Jack says, "The latter. You know how I always need that little bit of quiet time before a mission."

"Yeah, I understand."

"Did you spend time with Helen?"

"Yeah, she came over last night and stayed. We had a chance to talk about things we have been avoiding. It was good. I really never expected to love again like this, but it feels right and very good."

"I'm happy for you, and I think you are a very lucky man. You have found two good women in your life. That's a very rare thing you know, that right?"

"I know, and I know that I'm lucky. Now I want to get this thing over with, and I don't want to have to do this again in my life-time. I thought when I left New York that I was done with this kind of thing."

"Yeah, I know. After a while, this sort of thing begins to get to you."

"It sure does. Talking about me and Helen, I've got to ask when are you going to settle down?"

"I don't know, just never have met that right one, you know?"

"You need to stop long enough to give it a chance. You never stay in one place long enough."

"I know. I've been thinking about a career change but not sure to what yet."

"Like what? I don't see you as a police officer or a detective."

"I've been rolling it around in my head, and I thought about the FBI, just haven't looked into it yet."

"Really? Well, maybe in training at Quantico or in a field office?"

"I think more in a field office. I want to be as far away from Washington DC as possible."

"Well, you know there is this fairly big FBI office very close by in Atlanta."

"Yeah, I thought about that and after this is said and done, I might visit Atlanta's FBI office to see if there is anything there."

"Good. It would be nice having you close by. We might even get in a little fishing now and then."

Jack looked at Denton sideways. "You know it has been a really long time since I've been fishing, but I guess it's like riding a bike, you never forget how it just gets a little rusty."

They both laugh and about that time, the rest of the guys walk in.

They all go into the conference room and first talk about what they need to carry with them. Denton has already assembled everything they need from his office in the conference room, so the others go back out to their vehicles and bring in the equipment needed for this mission except for some of the weaponry that the Special Forces guys have with them. They look over what they have. Everyone will have a Kevlar vest for proper protection, and of course, all have rifles and plenty of ammo; also they have hand grenades. Jack and the guys from the FBI office have provided them all with means of communication. Billy and his group have brought two vehicles pulling trailers with each carrying two off-road four-wheelers. Denton's office has two off-road four-wheelers that Denton can pull behind his vehicle, and one of his officers has provided them with two more four-wheelers, giving them at least eight off-road four-wheelers to get them as close to the compound as possible. This will make it easier and faster to get to the compound or at least as close as they can get with vehicles.

They stop for a break around 7:00 p.m., and Denton has one of his officer's order in some pizzas and sandwiches for them to eat. They take their time knowing they still have a ways to go before heading out. Once they're done, they pull out the map and plat of the compound to start going over what they need to do for each group. They also need to look at where they want their backup to be and any extra help as far as routes out of North Carolina that anyone could take that might get by them from the compound. Of course, when Jack talked with the FBI office in Atlanta and arranged for backup, he also had put in place spotters on all major roads that could be accessed from the compound area, just in case of any unusual movement from the area occurred. This also gives them extra backup if needed once their attack has started.

Billy brings up something that he thought of that's very important to their not being detected or noticed when trying to get as close to the compound by vehicle. He knows of a place that they can go that hunters use, and it has a large barn there that they can pull their vehicles into it, so they can leave from there on their off-road vehicles. This will help just in case there is someone who's far away from the compound, watching for unusual movement. Hopefully it would look like just a group of hunters.

Now they're getting down to the nitty-gritty of this mission. They have all agreed that Billy and his guys will take out the six men posted outside the compound around the fence. Billy's guys have already put into place how they're going to coordinate taking out these six men.

John and his guys have been working on what part of the fence is the most vulnerable and have come up with halfway between the east and west end of the compound on the north side. There seems to be a little more space between the sentries posted outside the fence and more ground cover, making it easier to deal with the claymores there without being spotted. John and his five guys, as well as Denton and Jack, will enter the compound at this spot.

Billy and his five guys will take out the sentries all at the same time and let John know once that's done. By this time, John's man will have defused the claymore, and they will be ready to cut the fence. Billy and his guys will make their way to the entry point, always staying in contact with each other via the walkie-talkies they have. John and his group, along with Denton and Jack, will go ahead and enter. They will have the inferred equipment to determine which buildings there are warm bodies in, and they will split up accordingly, and once Billy and his guys are there, they will split up based on the communication they receive from John or Jack. It should still be dark; their thinking is it will be around 5:00 to 5:30 a.m. so that most of the people inside the compound will still be sleeping, making it easier to get the drop on them.

There will be at least one of John's guys with each group looking for any booby traps there might be. And of course, their rifles will have silencers on them. It's now 11:00 p.m., and they feel good about their plan, and Jack has talked with the FBI guys, and everyone, including the spotters, are in place and ready. Denton looks at everyone and says, "Okay, guys, there is coffee and donuts, and I think leftovers from dinner in the kitchen. Make yourselves at home and then find a comfortable place and get a little rest. We only have about three hours or less before we head out."

CHAPTER 52

It's now 2:00 a.m., Sunday, June 9, and Denton and the rest of the guys are ready to head out. Billy and his guys get into their two vehicles, pulling the trailers loaded with the four-wheelers they brought. John and his group of guys get into their vehicle that Denton has hooked up the fourth trailer his officer provided them, along with his two four-wheelers. Denton and Jack climb into his truck that's pulling the station's trailer with the other two four-wheelers. They have everything loaded needed for this mission. Denton lets Billy take the lead, along with his guys, then John in his vehicle, then Denton and Jack take up the rear.

It takes them about an hour and fifteen minutes to get to the hunter's cabin with the barn that Billy told them about. They unload the four wheelers and then pull the trucks and trailers into the barn. Then Billy's guys take three of the four-wheelers, and John and his guys take three of the four-wheelers, leaving two of the four-wheelers, one for Denton and one for Jack. This enables Denton and Jack to carry some of the equipment needed at the fence for John's guys.

It's a little slower going once they get into the area surrounding the three hundred acres where the compound lies. Once they get close, they abandon their vehicles and cover them with camouflage, hoping no one will spot them. Then they split up. Billy's guy's each head out in the direction need to rendezvous with the sentry each one is to take out. Their timing is essential to the operation being successful. Once each is in position, they have a code they will send over their walkie-talkie; this will allow them to syncretize their kills and also let John's group know this is done and ready for them to cut the fence.

John and his group are at the fence. Wallace is the bomb expert, so once they have reached the fence, he will disarm the claymore. Now they're ready for the signal from Billy and his guys. It takes about eight more minutes for each one of them to get into place once there, their signal goes out, and each sentry goes down. Al takes the laser they have brought to cut the electrified fence and proceeds to cut the fence while everyone else holds their breath. This is the part that was the most risk getting into the compound because without trying it first, it might not have worked. But Al is really good at what he does, so once the guys came back with the information they gathered from the recon, he was at least 85 percent sure it would work.

Now they have an opening large enough for them to pass through. Once inside, they stop beside one of the buildings to do a little more recon to see if they have sentries walking the compound and also to use the inferred equipment to see which buildings have people in them and just how many. They see no sentries and find only two buildings with people. One appears to be a bunkhouse, and it has at least twelve warm bodies. The other building seems to be a meeting place or a headquarters of sorts, and they can tell that there are four warm bodies sitting around a table and three others in two different rooms. These three warm bodies seem to be a sleep.

Before they decide to make a move, John sends out two of his men, Josh and Milton, to walk the perimeter inside the fence—just to make sure of any booby traps and other obstacles they might encounter. Within twenty-five minutes, they have returned, and Billy and his guys have joined them. They're ready to make their move. They split into three groups. Billy, Jason, Robby join Al and John; they head to the building that appears to be the bunkhouse where twelve guys seem to be asleep. Al takes the lead, so he can check for booby traps as they go. Jack, Denton, Wallace, Tommy, and Peter head toward the building that houses the other seven guys. Tommy takes the lead for this group to check for booby traps. Paul, Stanley, Josh, and Milton are going to go between the two buildings to give backup to either of the other two groups as needed and to make sure no one gets away.

All of sudden, one of the men from the second building steps out of one of the side doors to take a smoke and hears a sound. He turns and yells something and lights come on all over the place. Utter chaos ensues. The other three men that were in the same building come out shooting. At the same time, John's group hit the doors of the bunkhouse, and all hell breaks loose. The good thing about that building was that this was so unexpected that they were able to get the drop on these twelve men and prevent any of them from reaching their weapons.

Josh's group heads to the second building where the shooting started. Two of the guys headed behind the building, making sure no one came at them from that direction or got away. The rest went in to help Jack's group. They ended up killing the four guys that were awake that started the chaos and got to two of the men that were in one of the other rooms. Jack believes one is defiantly Abd al Bari, and in the room, they found him—they found what Jack believes are plans possibly of their target. But before they could get to the room that had just one person in it, he comes running out yelling something and has a grenade in his hand just as Jack is walking out of the room from where they found Abd al Bari. It goes off before anyone can do anything else. After the smoke settles, Denton realizes Jack is down, and of course, the one holding the grenade is in pieces.

Denton goes to Jack; Jack isn't moving. Denton is trying to assess his injuries. Denton tells Peter to look for anything they can use for a first aid kit and tells Tommy to go find John and get him to call for their backup and medical help. Peter finds what looks like a medic bag and takes it to Denton and helps Denton to determine where Jack has injuries.

John comes running in with Milton, who is the Special Forces acting medic as well, to see what they can do for Jack. Milton kneels beside Jack, and Denton slides out of the way. Milton looks Jack over and sees he's multiple injuries. Denton pushes the bag Peter found for him over to Milton, and he looks through the bag and pulls out bandages and starts methodically going from one injury to another, assessing the damage and trying to stop the bleeding.

Denton asks, "How bad is it?"

Milton replies, "It's not good. We need to get him to a hospital as soon as possible."

By this time, their backup has arrived, and they have radioed for a medivac. One arrives within ten minutes because they had the foresight to have one standing by not far from the area along with the backup. They do what they can for him on the ground but know they need him in a good trauma center as soon as possible. They decided to take him to Atlanta to Grady Memorial because it's the closes and best trauma center around. Denton really wants to go with him but knows he needs to stay here and help clean up this mess and make sure that nothing has already been put into play. The helicopter takes off, and the rest of the guys along with their backup for bombs and chemical weapons start their job of going through everything very carefully.

CHAPTER 53

It's now 9:00 a.m. on a Sunday, June 9, and Denton, along with John and his guys, have combed through everything inside the compound. They worked on this while Billy and his guys made sure that anyone with the extra backup didn't accidently set off any of the claymores around the perimeter. Denton and John are looking over the papers they found in the one room where Abd al Bari was sleeping and have realized what their target was. It was really scary knowing it was to be the National Mall of Washington DC and that they were going to not only use explosives but also chemical weaponry, and that they had planned to do this on July 4, which was less than a month away. Denton knew that this would be such a huge blow to the American people that he was having a hard time wrapping his head around it.

John said, "You know, I would never have believed that they would try something this big—this close to the 9/11 attack. But you have to give it to them. They don't let up on their beliefs and how they feel about our good old USA. I just hope that our powers that be see this as even a bigger wake-up call than they did 9/11 and make sure we get all areas needed secured and taken care of before they have another chance."

Denton replies, "Ain't that the truth, if they don't quit arguing amongst themselves and start working toward a solution to these terrorist attacks. Heaven help us all."

John's guys had found the truck already loaded with the bombs to be used, and they found in one of the other buildings the backpacks with the chemical weaponry already loaded as well. They were prepared to move at a moment's notices if necessary. Denton feels like they were really lucky they came across this before they had time to implement their plan, but his mind keeps going back to Jack, and he can't help but wonder how he is doing. They still have a lot of work ahead of them before they can head back to Mirror Lake, and he has no cell coverage up here, so no way to let Helen know they're okay or to check on Jack. But he knows that he will be back in Mirror Lake before the day is over and will be able to hold her in his arms.

It's now twelve noon, and there is still more work to be done inside the compound, but John tells Denton that he and Billy and Billy's guys can head back to Mirror Lake. John knows that Denton is really anxious to hear something on Jack's condition. And he, along with the rest of their people, has everything under control. John tells Denton they will see them back in Mirror Lake before the day is over. Denton, Billy, and his guys pick up the four-wheelers; Jason rides Jack's back as they head back to the trucks. Once back at the barn, Denton tells Billy and his guys that he can't thank them enough for all they have done and how much he appreciates it. He tells Billy to come in and see him on Monday.

Billy says, "Will do, but I'll call first. We do want to hear how Jack is doing as soon as you find out."

Denton says, "I'll let you know, and then we can set up a time for you to come into the office."

Billy and his guys load up their four-wheelers, and Denton loads his up and heads back to Mirror Lake.

Helen has been pacing all afternoon, and she's called the station at least three times since noon. She finally gives up and just goes to the station to wait. All the guys know her, of course, and they let her wait in Denton's office.

It's now 4:00 p.m. on Sunday, June 9, and Denton walks into the station. Helen hears the commotion and walks out of his office. Denton sees her and can't help but smile. All his officers are talking at the same time. He looks at them and says, "Give me just a few minutes, and I'll tell you everything." He walks over to Helen; they walk into his office, and he closes his door, and he takes her in his arms and holds on for dear life then looks into her face and kisses her softly. There are tears running down her face.

Once they let go, he tells her a little about what has happened and about Jack getting hurt and the need to call Atlanta to Grady to find out what is going on. He picks up his phone and calls his officer at the front desk and asks him to get Grady Memorial Hospital emergency room on the line for him. He and Helen are talking when his officer buzzes in and tells him he's got Grady emergency room on line 1. Denton picks up his phone and hits line 1 and says, "This is Denton Gage, the sheriff of Mirror Lake, North Carolina. I'm calling checking on status of a man by the name of Jack Abrams, who was brought in by military medivac earlier today. Is there anything you can tell me?"

The person on the other end of the line says, "Please hold for just a minute."

In a couple of minutes, a man came on the line that's in administration with the hospital and asks again who Denton was.

Denton replies, "I'm Denton Gage, the sheriff of Mirror Lake, North Carolina, calling regarding the status of Jack Abrams. He was brought to Grady earlier today by military medivac. He is with Homeland Security, and I was with him when he was injured."

The man on the other end of the line says, "My name is Wilson Hardy. I'm the head of emergency services with Grady, and I'm sorry we are not supposed to give out information unless it's a family member."

Denton is about to get angry but holds his temper. "I understand that, but as far as I know, he has no family, and I've known and worked with this man for many years. Now I want an update on his conditions now, and I'll not take no for an answer."

Mr. Hardy clears his throat and says, "He is in surgery, and that's about all I know. He was in really bad shape when he got here, and I know that our staff is doing the best they can to do under the circumstances. If you'll give me your contact information as soon as we have more, I'll let you know."

Denton gives him his name and his cell before hanging up.

Helen looks at Denton's distraught face and says, "I can call Margaret and ask her to go over to the hospital and sit so she can get back to us as soon as possible. And we can get ready and head to Atlanta within an hour and be at Grady in about two hours."

Denton just looks at her in amazement; how she can take any situation no matter how stressful it is and calm the waters. He says to her, "Yes, please call Margaret, and I'll change clothes. I've got something here that will work. You don't mind going with me to Atlanta? I mean, what about your mother?"

"I'll first call Margaret, and then I'll call mother. She will be fine, and as soon as you are ready, we will head out."

Denton just thinks how much he loves this woman and doesn't know what he would do without her.

CHAPTER 54

Helen has called Margaret and tells her briefly what has happened and asks if she will go to Grady and check on Jack and call her or Denton's cell once she's any update. Of course, Margaret says no problem, and she will be waiting at the hospital for them to arrive. Then Helen calls her mother and lets her know what she is doing and has one of their neighbors go over to stay with her mom for the night. She knows they will not be back before tomorrow or the next day. Denton walks back into his office; he's showered and changed and also briefed his men on what went down and where he is going. They, of course, will hold down the fort for him.

Helen looks at him and says, "Okay, you ready to head out? I've taken care of mother and have talked with Margaret, and she is headed to Grady as we speak."

Denton takes Helen in his arms again and kisses her and says, "I don't know what I would do without you."

Helen smiles. "You don't have to worry about that. I'm here for the long haul."

They head out the door, but before they leave, Denton tells his officer in charge to let John with Special Forces know where he's gone and to ask him to stick around if he can or to call him on his cell.

It takes them about two-and-half hours to reach Grady. It's now 8:15 p.m., and they walk into the waiting room for surgery. Margaret gets up to greet them. "Hi, guys." She looks at Denton with sad eyes and says, "How you holding up, Denton?"

Denton says, "I'm fine. Have you heard anything on Jack?"

"Yes, he is out of surgery and in ICU. Other than that, they're saying the next forty-eight hours will tell more."

Denton runs his hand down his face and sighs. Helen takes Denton's hand and says, "He made it through surgery, Denton. That's huge. Now all we can do is be here for him and pray for him."

Denton knows this but really needs to see him. He looks at Margaret and says, "Will they let anyone see him?"

"Well, they do have visiting hours for ICU, but I'm not sure if they will let anyone other than family in. It was not easy getting the info I got from them."

Denton knew this because it was the same when he called. He decides to go check and see if they would let him in to see Jack. Helen and Margaret stay in the waiting room and wait for his return. Denton comes back and says, "They have agreed to let me see him for just a minute or two. They say he is in a medical induced coma, so he will not know I'm there. But I've got to see him, so are you guys okay with waiting?"

Helen replies, "Sure, I've no place to be, and if Margaret wants to leave, she can. I can get us to her place from here."

Denton says, "Thanks," and sits down with them in the waiting room.

In just a few minutes, someone comes to let Denton know that he can now see Jack. Denton tells them he will be back in just a few. He is escorted back to ICU to Jacks room. They tell him only three minutes no more. Denton walks in and takes Jacks hand and says, "Sorry, Jack, this was not supposed to happen. But good news, we got the sons of bitches, and we found everything we needed. We got them before they could complete their plans. Also we got that asshole, Abd al Bari, and he will be locked up, and we will throw away the key. He will never be able to hurt another American again. Just know I'm here and will be here for you until I know you are out of the woods."

The nurse comes to the door and quietly knocks on the door frame, and Denton puts Jack's hand down and walks out of the room.

Back in the waiting room, he tells Helen and Margaret that he wants to stay at the hospital but tells them to go to Margaret's and get some rest. Helen didn't want to leave him, but he insisted that she go. So Helen and Margaret go back to Margaret's to rest. Denton talks with John over the phone and gives him an update on Jack. He lets him know he will be in Atlanta for several days at least.

John said, "That's fine. We can talk later. I hope Jack does okay, just keep me informed." John also lets Denton know that he left the four-wheelers with his officers.

Denton told him thanks, and he would be in touch.

CHAPTER 55

Helen and Margaret are back at Helen's condo. Margaret asks Helen, "Are you hungry? I bet you guys didn't stop once you left Mirror Lake, so I know you haven't eaten."

Helen says, "Yeah, I guess a little, and you are right, we didn't stop. Denton was anxious to get here. Plus, he or I neither one was hungry."

"I'll make you a quick sandwich, and you can grab a beer out of the fridge."

"Thanks. I really appreciate all you have done and are doing now. It really means a lot to me and Denton especially, Jack is like a brother to him. He was so worried about him. I knew that the only way he could handle this was to be here with Jack no matter the outcome."

"Hey, what I've done isn't anything, and what are families for. I've got a feeling Denton will be part of the family before we know it anyway."

Helen smiles. "I'm not sure how soon or even if that will happen, but I do know one thing, he is very important to me, and I think I am to him. So I'm good with taking things slow." Helen is sitting at the kitchen island with her beer, and Margaret hands over her sandwich. Helen says, "Thanks. This looks good"

Margaret sits on a stool next to Helen and says, "Okay, now tell me what has gone on and how Jack got hurt."

Helen tells her about everything that Denton and Jack had been able to find out about this Mr. Amjad—of course, she already knew some of it. Helen also tells her about Jack contacting a group with Special Forces, how they had come to Mirror Lake with a group from the FBI Atlanta office to work on things, how the Special Forces guys had done recon on the hunt club, how Denton contacted Billy Bob Johnson, and he, along with five guys he had served with in the military, met with them and help carry out their mission. She also told her how Jack got hurt. That one of the terrorist had a hand grenade and walked into the room where they were, and it went off, and how Jack was the closest one to this terrorist, so his injuries were from shrapnel.

Margaret was in shock. She says, "I can't believe they found out all of this, worked up a plan, and were able to stop a huge terrorist attack. This really is huge, and you say this all came about because of Denton and just not having a good feeling about this Mr. Amjad and Mr. Sommeren?"

"Yeah, I guess going through the 9/11 attacks the way he did, and his loss makes him look at the world differently. And of course, when he met them at the gallery opening, and he just happened to be standing close to Henry Mason and Gordon Grover and overheard their conversation, it just start him thinking that something didn't sound right. So he took it from there, and I think that's when he contacted Jack."

"Do they know where these terrorist were planning to attack?"

"If I understood Denton, their target was to be the National Mall of Washington DC, and they planned to attack on July 4. But you can't tell anyone about this, okay?"

"Are you serious? The National Mall of Washington? Oh my god, that would be devastating to the moral of the American people and on the fourth of July. I can't even imagine the loss of life. That place would be packed on the fourth of July."

"Yes, you are right, and they want this to stay quiet because it would do nothing but cause panic and also add to racial profiling. That's something they don't want to happen. There is enough fear out there already to add to it. Denton says that this was just a terrorist cell that had been dormant for years that they don't believe they're any part of the group that planned 9/11. He said this Mr. Amjad, aka Abd al Bari, had been underground for a long time, and they were not even sure if he was alive. I guess he decided that this was his big opportunity to make his mark on the world. Mr. Sommeren didn't really come up on their radar at all, so they're not sure yet how he fits into all of this. But Denton believes he was the person that had the hand grenade that caused Jack's injuries, and of course, that means Mr. Sommeren is dead."

"Well, you can assure Denton I'll not mention this to anyone. I know how scared I am just knowing about all of this. I would not want to be the person that scared the whole nation. We have had enough of that."

"Thanks again for all of this and for listening to me, and I know that we don't have to worry about this going anywhere else."

By this time, Helen has finished her sandwich and beer and yawns big. Margaret says, "Let's go to bed and get some rest. We will get back to the hospital in the morning and take Denton some breakfast."

"That sounds good. I need to give Denton a call and check on him." Helen heads to Margaret's guest room and gives Denton a call.

Denton says, "Hi, I thought you would be in bed by now?"

"No, Margaret fixed me a sandwich, and we talked about what has happened. She wanted to know how Jack got hurt. But don't worry, she knows not to talk about this to anyone. And I can tell you if anyone can keep a secret, it's Margaret."

Denton half-heartily laughed and said, "I'm not worried about Margaret."

Helen asks, "Have you heard anything else about Jack."

"No, everything seems to be the same."

"Did you eat anything?"

"No, I've had some coffee, not really hungry. You need to get some rest, and I'll see you tomorrow."

"I will, and you try to get some rest. Call me if you need me, and I'll bring you breakfast in the morning."

"That sounds great. See you then. I love you."

"I love you too. Please try to rest."

CHAPTER 56

It's now Monday, June 10. Helen and Margaret head out to the hospital. They stop and pick up breakfast for all three of them. Denton is sitting in the waiting room with a cup of coffee in his hand when they walk in. Denton rises and walks over to Helen and leans down and gives her a kiss then says, "I'm glad you are here and have brought breakfast because I'm really hungry. I realized this morning that I haven't eaten since Saturday around 7:00 p.m. You know, with all the adrenaline rush and with everything, you just don't get hungry. But I believe it has caught up with me."

Helen says, "I'm sure it has. Did you get any rest, and have you heard anything or seen Jack this morning?"

Denton, as they all sit at a table in the waiting room and start eating their breakfast, says, "I did rest a little. I was so tired. But no, I haven't heard anything other than he is still in a medical induced coma, and they might try later today to bring him out of it. That's if his vitals are all good."

"Well, that sounds promising. It surely means things are going well."

"I believe so. I really want to see his eyes open and be able to talk to him."

They sit around the table and finish their breakfast and talk for a little while.

Margaret says, "Well, if you guys are okay here, I'm going to head to the office for a little while. I don't have anything working right now that can't wait for a bit, but I want to look at things and think about how to close out anything that has to do with this Mr. Sommeren and Mr. Amjad."

Denton looks at Margaret. "Well, why don't you get everything together, and hopefully Jack, at least within the next two weeks, will be able to work with me and you go over how to go about closing out yours and Helen's dealings with these two men. This will allow us to do it without having to bring your whole firm into the loop."

"That sounds good to me, and I'll be back over here. Let's say around 3:00 p.m. with lunch, if that's okay."

Denton and Helen say in unison, "That sounds great."

Helen gets up and throws away their papers and walks Margaret out.

When Helen walks back into the waiting room, Denton is on his phone with one of his officers in charge. Denton appears to be angry. Helen waits until he was off the phone and then asks, "What is going on? Is everything all right at Mirror Lake?"

"Yeah, it's just that damn Henry Mason. He is giving them hell at the office. He wants to know where I'm at and what has been going on. He is threatening to call the governor of North Carolina."

"Well, let him. Didn't you tell me that the governor was briefed on this whole situation?"

"Yeah, it just makes me mad that he is in the position he is in and seems to be so stupid."

"Well, what can I say, but his family have been a big part of Mirror Lake forever and really no one else wanted the job. You have to realize that no one pays attention to Henry, and they never have."

Denton laughs a little. "I guess I'll eventually get use to small town life, but I'll say I'm not sure I'll ever get use to Henry Mason."

Helen smiles. "I know he is an acquired taste unfortunately. But know this, he has no real power. He has to answer to the board of commissioners as you have seen, and they're much smarter than he is, and they know what they want. So I don't think you have a problem."

They have been sitting there for a while when a nurse from ICU comes out and tells Denton that they have reduced the medication that has kept Jack in a medical induced coma, and it appears he is coming around. She asks Denton if he would like to come in and be there as he comes around. Denton looks at Helen, and she says, "Go be with Jack, I'll be right here."

Denton leans down and kisses Helen and says, "I love you and see you in a little while."

Helen just smiles as he walks away with the nurse.

Once in Jack's room, they ask Denton to stand back at the doors opening while the nurses and doctor work with him to see if they can arouse him from this coma-like state. Denton does as they ask and just watches. The doctor stands on one side, and the nurse on the other; the nurse is gradually administering medication through Jack's intravenous line; this is to help bring him out of this coma-like state. As they work with Jack, he starts coming around slowly but finally opens his eyes. Of course, he isn't fully aware of his surrounding and keeps slipping back into sleep. This goes on for a while, and the doctor explains that it might take a couple hours for him to come completely around, but it looks very good. His vital signs have stayed stable. They let Denton know that he can sit with Jack for a while and see what happens. They feel it would be good for Jack to see a friendly face when he opens his eyes and can focus. Denton ask the nurse to let Helen know that it might be a while before he is back out there with her.

It's now 3:00 p.m. on Monday, June 10, and Margaret walks back into the waiting room. She only sees Helen and hopes that's a good sign. Margaret approaches Helen and says, "Hi, sis, everything okay? Where is Denton?"

"He is in with Jack. They have taken away the drugs that was creating the medical induced coma and is trying to bring him back to the real world. They thought it would be good for Denton to be with him, so he sees a friendly face once he opens his eyes and can focus."

"That sounds very promising. How long has it been?"

"He's been in with Jack about two hours."

"Well, are you hungry? I brought lunch. Mind you, it's just sandwiches."

Helen says, "Yes, I'm hungry, and sandwiches are great. I don't know when Denton will come out, but he can eat then."

They sit at the table in the waiting room and eat lunch and talk.

CHAPTER 57

Margaret and Helen are sitting in the waiting room, talking when Denton walks back into the room. They both stand and notice that Denton is smiling. Helen walks up to Denton. "Well, how is he? Were you able to talk with him?"

Denton says, "Yes, just briefly. He kind of keeps slipping in and out of sleep. They say that's normal, but they feel he is going to make a full recovery."

Helen and Margaret, in unison, says, "That's great."

Denton says, "I really haven't been able to tell him anything, not really sure how much he understands at this point. He does know who I am, and that's good."

Helen says, "Well, everything sounds good, but I'm guessing it's going to take a while."

"Yeah, they say he will be in the hospital for at least two weeks, but they plan on moving him to a private room tomorrow if all goes well."

Margaret says, "Great. Now I know you have to be hungry. I've got you lunch over here, so you come and eat and talk with Helen. I plan to go back to work for a while and see you around five-thirty or six this afternoon?"

Helen says, "That sounds good. Don't work too hard and call if anything changes. We could get a cab over to your place if need be."

"That's not necessary. I'll see you guys later." Margaret leaves, and Denton and Helen sit and talk while Denton eats his lunch.

Later that afternoon, Denton goes back in with Jack; he appears to be a little more alert. Denton is glad to see this because he called Denton by name as he walked into his room. Denton looks at Jack and says, "Sorry, dude, but you look like hell."

Jack smiles a little. "You don't look much better. And I think I've got a better reason for the way I look."

Denton takes Jack's hand. "You know, we were really worried about you. You got hit really hard. Do you remember what happened?"

"Yeah, a little. I remember where we were, and that I saw a large flash of light as I walked out of the room I was in, and then everything with black."

"Well, first, we got all of them and all of their plans before they were able to execute anything. Also we got Abd al Bari alive, so he will go away forever and never be able to harm another American."

Jack smiles as best he can. "That's great. Were we able to disarm everything they had?"

"Yeah, thanks to your good thinking and having the kind of backup we had. They had a truck loaded with explosives and backpacks loaded with light bulb's full of chemicals that were planned to kill a lot of people."

Jack couldn't believe what he was hearing. "What was their target? Were we able to determine that?"

"Yeah, it was to be the National Mall of Washington. They planned to drive the truck with the explosives into the west end, and three guys were going to walk into the east end with the chemical weaponry, and they planned this to happen on July 4."

Jack asks, "What about the other guys? Anyone else hurt?"

"No, everyone is okay. You were the only lucky one that gets the attention."

Jack closes his eyes for just a minute then says, "It's good you have such great instincts, or we would never have done this before this tragedy happened."

"I'm not sure of that, but I believe there was a good reason I choose Mirror Lake. I was at the right place at the right time."

"I think there were two good reasons you were at the right place at the right time." He smiles and says, "Helen O'Keefe Coleman just might be the best reason."

They both smile and just sit for a while. Jack needs to rest, and now he knows the outcome of their situation.

CHAPTER 58

It's now Tuesday, June the eighteenth, and Denton and Helen have been back and forth a number of times between Mirror Lake and Atlanta. Jack is doing extremely well and is bugging the doctors to let him out of the hospital. He and Denton have had a number of debriefings with Homeland Security and the FBI regarding the situation in North Carolina.

The head of Homeland Security was extremely happy with the way things turned out, and the apprehension of Abd al Bari was a really big deal. They hope it will go a long way toward the fight against terrorism. They have also talked with John in Special Forces and thanked them for all they have done. They let Jack know they would not have had it any other way they were proud to be of service.

Things have gotten back to normal in Mirror Lake. Helen is staying busy with the gallery. She was glad that they were able to work out something through the state department for her to keep the items that she had received from Mr. Amjad for display only. It adds depth to her gallery. Margaret was able to close out her accounts for Mr. Sommeren and Mr. Amjad without having to explain to the partners in Gilpin, Grays and Connors what had taken place in North Carolina and her part in it. This made her life a little easier. Also she's been going to the hospital every day and spending time with Jack. She's found that he is a very interesting person to be around.

Helen and Denton have carried on with their lives and are very happy for things to be back to normal—at least as normal as usual around Mirror Lake and having to deal with Henry Mason.

EPILOGUE

It's July the fourth, 2002, in Mirror Lake. Denton and Helen have arranged for a big celebration at Denton's place down by the lake. Of course, all of Helen's family included but not limited to Pat and David Martin from Cumming, Georgia; Melonie and Donald Steedwell from Eastman, Georgia; and of course, Margaret O'Keefe from Atlanta, Georgia, along with their mother, Mildred O'Keefe, were there.

They have also included Jack Abrams, whom—over the last few weeks—has become a fixture in their lives. The doctors released him a little earlier than planned only because he was able to stay in Atlanta near the hospital. Margaret had opened her home to him, and he stayed in her guest room. They have become quite close. They found they have a lot in common.

Denton also made sure that Billy, Jason, Paul, Robby, Stanley, and Peter were there. He had extended an invitation to John and his guys, but unfortunately, they were away on assignment.

Denton had set up a number of picnic tables and chairs all around the area and had a number of grills going. With the help of Billy and his friends, they were all attended to while everyone visited.

Helen and Margaret were sitting in a swing, and Helen looks at Margaret and ask, "How are things going with you and Jack? I mean, I think I see something there, correct?"

Margaret smiles. "I think so. We haven't really talked about it. He hasn't even kissed me, but we do like a lot of the same things and seem to enjoy each other's company."

"That sounds good. I know that Denton says he is a good man and thinks very highly of him."

Not far away from them stands Denton at a grill, and Jack is sitting in a chair next to him. Denton looks at Jack. "Okay, what gives?"

"What are you talking about?"

"You know, Margaret? What's going on between you two?"

"Nothing. She's been really nice to let me stay with her and take me back and forth to the hospital when I needed to go."

Denton says, "That's not all. So what else is going on?"

"Nothing, I'll say I really like her. We have a lot in common, and she is just a beautiful woman. I'll tell you this, I've talked with the FBI Office in Atlanta several times, and they do have a position available that I'm really looking at."

"That's great, and I hope that means that just maybe Margaret has a part in that decision as well."

Jack says, "Well, her being in Atlanta certainly does hurt."

Everyone has enjoyed a good meal and being together on this momentous day as it winds down. They all gather around the lake either in chairs or on blanks, and Denton and Helen sit in their favorite spot in the swing and watch the Mirror Lake annual fireworks. It's a perfect end to a perfect day.

ABOUT THE AUTHOR

Myra lives in a small North Georgia town. She has one adult son, married and two grandsons. She is a dog lover and has a dog named Leo. She retired from accounting in 2015 to take care of her ailing husband, who died in 2017, after forty-three years of marriage. She has always been an avid reader; now writing is a new passion in her life. She spends quality time with her family, and her private time is divided between reading and writing, and Leo and friends. She also loves her time outdoors whether it's just working in her yard, visiting nearby parks, and trips to the North Georgia mountains.